Island Pursuits

Heather Rodney-Diaz

CRIMSON
ROMANCE
Avon, Massachusetts

Published by
Crimson Romance
an imprint of F+W Media, Inc.
10151 Carver Road, Suite 200
Blue Ash, Ohio 45242

www.crimsonromance.com

Dedication

To my amazing husband Trevor, thank you for your un-ending patience and unwavering support.

To my family for your belief in me, encouragement, and support from the start.

To my military friends around the globe fighting the good fight and for making this book even more special. Thank you for your steadfast courage and sacrifices every day so that we may feel safer: Police Corporal Miguel Anthony Edwards, Police Constable Junior Nisbett and Specialist Michael Forrester, Unit 1bct 3-6 Field Artillery Golf Company, Fort Drum, New York.

Chapter 1

Capital City of Port of Spain, Trinidad

Okay, so this wasn't exactly how Cory Phillips envisioned her New Year to start. In fact, this was just plain ridiculous. It had been a good party until that drunken idiot had started pawing at her. But *this?* In the parking lot outside the hotel, all she saw was the space where her car was supposed to be parked. She stood there and argued with herself over the correct spot before going back into the hotel to get security. They walked about the car park with her but there were no signs of her car anywhere. That was when the shock finally kicked in. And that was when she called Jay.

"You just can't be without me for a few hours, eh, Cory?" Jay asked as soon as his metallic-blue Subaru stopped outside the hotel. He'd been at another party in the city with his family, enjoying their New Year ritual.

Since Trinidad was an energy-efficient island rich in oil and natural gas, many of the world's largest multinationals set up offices here. Cory and Jay had gone to work for Petronas de España TT on the very same day and had become close work buddies, despite their differing job duties—Cory was an assistant manager in the corporate communications department while Jay was an accountant.

"You look handsome," Cory commented as she got in next to him. Jay's crisp white shirt and tie complemented his fine dark chocolate skin tone and handsome features.

"Seriously, Cory! You need to find yourself a man this year, so you can leave me to get my groove on in peace," Jay let out in one long, quick breath.

"Are you done?"

"Yeah. Well, you know I just had to say that. Happy New Year by the way." Jay stretched his lanky frame over and gave Cory a peck on the cheek.

"Happy New Year to you, too . . . but it's not happy. They stole my car, Jay," Cory sulked. "I can't believe this. From the hotel's parking lot? This is madness!"

"Where're the others?" he asked.

"Inside. Setting the dance floor on fire," Cory said. At the last minute, she'd come to this swanky party with her girlfriends, who had brought dates. But tonight Cory had just wanted to escape the forced revelry. And now her car was missing.

"So what did the hotel say?"

"That they're not responsible and to go and make a report at the nearest police station," she said.

"Well, of course they'll have a disclaimer, Cory."

"God . . . if I could only see those idiots now," Cory moaned.

When Jay reached the police station and they got out, there was a bit of commotion as some policemen were dragging in a struggling and cursing male prisoner. At any other time, this scene would have been completely hilarious to her and Jay. She didn't see the humor at the moment.

"Cory, go in. I have to make a call first," Jay said. He always did that, never wanting her listening in on his conversations. And Cory understood why for the most part. As she stood there, she cringed, remembering why she hated this place so much. Having to deal with the police yet again was just too much for her to handle. She took a deep breath in the yard, trying to calm herself.

One of the soldiers standing outside was quick in opening the door for her. He motioned for her to step inside.

"Good morning, ma'am," he said to her.

Instantly, his voice intrigued Cory. It was very soft but deep. And it was different, thickly laced and heavily accented. It didn't take a degree in linguistics to detect his American accent; the man couldn't be a local. When their eyes connected and his inquiring ones pierced hers, she felt dazed. Okay, so gorgeous was an understatement. This man was fine as hell with his light honey-toned skin, surely the smoothest she'd ever seen on a man. He was clean shaven and sported a very low hair cut and he was looking at her intently . . . expectantly.

"Good morning," Cory finally found her manners, snapping out of her daze. She felt flushed. Why was she suddenly feeling so exposed? Only then did she become self-conscious of her outfit. She was wearing a floor-length, form-fitting, low-cut back dress to make a stolen car report at a police station.

As she moved past him, her breasts ever so lightly brushed the arm he had up holding the door for her. Cory felt an instant electric jolt coursing through her entire body. It was a raw and intensely delicious heat, slowly but carefully ravaging her entire body, hardening her nipples. Outside was a bit chilly but the air between them now was just sizzling. And this man definitely noticed it, too.

"Thank you," she hurriedly managed to say again.

"My pleasure, ma'am," he said as he smiled down at her.

Yes, that was definitely pleasurable. Cory found he had a beautiful and sexy smile. But what had her worried was that one touch from this strange man and her body sprang to life, responding to him like that. Now, that was a totally new experience for her.

Maybe she really needed to take Jay's advice and throw a good man in the mix. She did miss the closeness shared between a man and woman. But was there anything remotely close to a good man out there? She had had her fill of the arguments, the tears, and the broken hearts. And who had time for a relationship these days, anyway?

*

As Adrian Mendez smiled down into the island goddess's perplexed face, he knew there was a God. Adrian had surely seen a lot for his thirty-two years on this planet, but this just now, never in his lifetime! Just a few minutes ago he had chased, caught, and felt like mercilessly pulverizing that young gang-banger. He had been on edge all day long. He even had doubts about his purpose for being on this island. Now he felt like he'd finally gotten a sign from the heavens that made his extremely long shift all worth it.

Adrian just wasn't prepared for these huge eyes with the longest eyelashes he believed he'd ever seen and which most definitely looked real enough to him. Elegantly arched eyebrows and seductive lips perfected this goddess's face. Now as she walked through the door, the view of her more-than-ample behind riveted his attention.

Adrian's eyes had been fixed on her since she'd gotten out the car and as she walked closer her beauty literally took his breath away. The sexy dress hugged her every curve, swaying and moving to the rhythm of her voluptuous hips. A very low and breathless sound unexpectedly escaped his lips as she moved past him. She made her way to the counter to speak to an officer and the very male-friendly, feminine curves of her body screamed out his name. Suddenly, Adrian felt so thirsty. He made his way inside to the water fountain. There, pure male instinct directed his eyes to slowly rove all over her again.

Adrian wondered who this woman was. Was she a victim of some sort of crime? It would really be a shame if she was. But she just looked so out of place here. Women like her certainly rarely ever showed up here for whatever reason. Then again, why would they? This area was plagued with drugs, gang wars, and any other criminal element you could name. And this station was known for its high levels of corruption and its location was in one of the most depressed areas of the country.

Adrian stared at the wild, crazy curls of her hair. They fell to the middle of her back and made her even more alluring to him. And that form-fitting black dress hugged what seemed to be the most perfect derriere and Adrian was so tempted to reach out and touch that. And for the life of him, all his thoughts now lingered on what type of underwear she was wearing under that lovely dress. If any?

Was it the lacy kind or a thong? Was it black just like her dress? Adrian found himself instantly turned on by this woman. What was it about this job that heightened your sexual appetite? Apparently, you were always horny. Probably the adrenaline rush caused by the stress, Adrian figured. He had to admit, nothing relaxed him better than some good action between the sheets. Now he needed some more water after that thought.

Stupidly, he was trying in vain to press the button on the fountain for the water to come up, all the while still paying homage to her luscious form. It was hopeless, he knew, but he just couldn't take his eyes off her. Not even when the cold water splashed all over his face and some even got up his nose, did Adrian's eyes move. The coldness shocked him but he welcomed it. He needed to mind his own business.

Then just like that, the man she'd driven up with came up to her in his too-tight-fitting (for Adrian's tastes) shirt and pants and protectively covered her shoulders with his jacket. Oh, so now he wanted to cover her up, Adrian inwardly fumed. Why didn't the jerk do that in the first place instead of letting her walk into a police station all by herself and exposed like that at this hour? But Adrian figured whoever the guy was talking to on his cell phone was obviously more important to him than the woman was. He knew if she were his woman, he'd never take his eyes off her.

*

When Cory was finished giving her report to the officer for the tenth time, she and Jay quickly headed out the door.

"You had an admirer back there," Jay announced when they were safely outside.

"Oh, yeah. Who?" Cory asked.

"One heavily armed and pissed off-looking soldier."

"Oh! The cute one with the American accent?" Cory asked with an unmistakably urgent interest in her voice.

"I don't know. He didn't speak to me. But it looked like he was having a very serious conversation with your ass because his eyes never moved from there."

Despite her depressed mood, Cory burst out laughing. "He was looking at my ass? Seriously? Hmm, little does he know?"

"Seriously, Cory, you need a man, okay?" was Jay's response to that.

"Only one? You think?" Cory asked in mock exaggeration. "With my drought, I probably need more like four."

"And I already feel sorry for all of them," Jay winced.

When they settled back into the car only then did he ask her, "So you'll be okay, right Ri-Ri?" Jay was the only person who called her by that name and only when he was in his rare brotherly moment.

"When I get my car back, I'll be."

"Well then, you better start praying hard, Miss Nice Ass."

Chapter 2

The whiff of a horrific stench emanating from her surroundings outside hit her hard, bringing Cory head-on with her immediate dismal reality. She was dreaming no more. Here she was, back again in this grimy and dreaded place she loathed so much.

It had been two days since the theft of her car and she hadn't heard anything. Now, Cory was here and ready to do battle. She needed her car back. It was amazing how public transportation could immediately snap you out of it.

Jay had been with her the first time she had come in to report the matter; today she was all alone. Cory pushed the door open and stepped inside the station's waiting area. She walked up to the counter and began speaking to a male police officer on the whereabouts of her car.

It didn't take long before she started screaming. Cory knew she could be over- dramatic at times but she totally lost it when the officer showed complete disinterest in helping her. Drama was a skill she most definitely got from her father. He had the literary background, being a high school teacher of literature and language for the past thirty-two years. So if drama helped her cause today, hats off to his literary genius and years of coaching.

Anger, disbelief, and frustration came hot and fast. As if she didn't have enough to deal with these days!

*

As Adrian opened the side door to the waiting room of the station, two things caught his attention. The first thing he noticed was her legs. What seemed like miles and miles of a beautifully created, well-formed masterpiece. Then her voice. Well, it was more like a high-pitched scream actually. She leaned over the counter animatedly talking to Stewart. As Adrian's eyes studied this wondrous sight some more, they met that tight, perfect ass and those wild curls. Adrian couldn't believe his eyes. His New Year object of desire had returned.

The waiting area was probably the calmest he ever saw it. The place was usually a madhouse around this time of day. The other people waiting certainly didn't look like her. There was one woman sitting with a bad weave and a gold tooth flashing in her mouth, maybe the reason she couldn't keep it closed. Add in the ton of baby powder heavily caked to her neckline and huge capital G gold earrings dangling from her ears. Another young man was standing speaking to a female officer, his pants uncomfortably sagging under his butt. These were the regulars they had at this station.

He was leaving to go out for lunch in the city. His training exercise with some of the officers here was finished until afternoon. Adrian had been assigned to a special task force for a little over two years now, an elite military unit introduced by the government of the island. Their mandate: to respond to all extremely violent crimes, especially gang violence and firearm offenses.

Adrian was starving but her presence had stopped him dead in his tracks.

The conversation she was having with Stewart was heatedly escalating. She was holding her head between her hands and shaking it in total disbelief. It was about time he found out who this upset goddess was. It was obvious her boyfriend hadn't tagged along this time.

He walked over in their direction, forgetting all about lunch for the moment. As Adrian approached, she paid him no mind. Stewart's sour expression clearly signaled he wasn't a happy camper and Adrian figured his butting in would just aggravate the man even more. Policemen and soldiers didn't necessarily get along well here but that was a risk he was willing to take.

"Excuse me, ma'am, is everything okay over here?" Adrian asked her.

"No! Everything is not okay," she screamed at the top of her lungs, without even looking his way. Then she stopped.

She looked at him, seemed to recognize him, and stood speechless for a moment. Then she began explaining to him, "I came to find out if my car was found yet, but nobody here seem to care enough to tell me anything."

It was hard for Adrian to concentrate on what she was saying. She had the most exotic brown skin and her wild hair just tempted his fingers to smooth back the curls from her face. Undoubtedly, he would be slapped silly if he attempted that move. But that didn't stop him from enjoying the view. Those high heels just topped it off for him. Adrian was definitely happy he had intervened here. Since their first encounter he had been totally captivated by this woman.

This time, he was taking in all of her from much closer. Her cleavage strained the fitted white blouse she was wearing under the tailored gray jacket, her breasts obviously screaming to be let out. Maybe it was the belt on her tiny waistline making them out to be so obvious to his hungry gaze and emphasizing to him their luscious ripeness.

"So can anybody in this place tell me something?" Cory started to cry.

It was her tears that finally brought Adrian's mind back down to earth. That was when it hit him. The reason why he had decided to come back after twenty years of life in America. This woman made it all clear once again. He wanted to help people. Growing up, he wanted to be nothing else but a soldier, just like his father was. And to this day, Adrian could never imagine himself doing anything else but that. So he tried to do what he was trained for; to serve proudly.

"So your car was stolen the other night?" Adrian asked her.

"Yes." He could see she was trying to pull herself together now, trying to calm down.

"What's your name?"

"Cory. Cory Phillips."

Adrian nodded. *Pretty name.* "Okay, Cory. Let me see if I can help." He turned his attention for the first time to the officer standing behind the desk.

"So Stewart, what's the status on this?" Adrian asked.

A pissed-off looking Stewart replied, "I was just telling her I don't know and Franklin isn't here right now."

"Franklin is the investigating officer?" Adrian asked next.

"Yeah."

"And he has all the required information, right?"

"Not that I see this is any of your business, Mendez. But yes, he should. I'm trying to tell her this but it's like she doesn't understand English."

"*What?*" Cory blurted. "Well, maybe you should try telling me in Spanish because I can understand that!"

Stewart was raising his voice at Cory again. "Because like you're hard of understanding something as simple as this, lady."

"Me!" Cory screamed. "Well, if this is so simple, you all would've found my car already, wouldn't you?"

Stewart glared at her. Cory glared right back at him.

"Stewart. Enough!" Adrian wanted to quell the disaster that was about to erupt here. It was apparent that this conversation wasn't going anywhere. The woman looked like she was about to floor Stewart, explode from anger, or both. "I'll handle this," Adrian announced. "Ma'am, please come with me."

"Mendez, yuh crazy? Yuh can't do this. This is not your jurisdiction. Yuh cannot walk in here and do as yuh please. You're here to conduct a training exercise," Stewart's voice also reached a high-pitched screech. "This is police work, so leave it to us."

Although Stewart was right, Adrian casually ignored him. Soldiers were just there to assist but Adrian didn't like the tone he was using with this woman at all.

"Stewart, I said I'll handle this," Adrian firmly restated without even raising his voice. He only shouted and cussed when was absolutely necessary. "Ma'am, please come with me."

Chapter 3

Cory smiled inwardly when she heard the long slew of colorful expletives from Stewart as she turned away from the desk to follow the man he called Mendez. She didn't know who Mendez was yet but if she was going on looks and politeness, he was clearly tipping the scale. She followed him through a side door, down a corridor and then into a room that looked like some sort of classroom.

"Have a seat please, ma'am," he offered. Cory gladly took the seat, resting her expensive handbag protectively on the desk in front of her.

He sat on the edge of the same desk, looking down at her. He pulled out a couple of tissues from a box sitting on the desk and handed them to her. "Urr, you have some stuff running down your face, ma'am," he said.

"Oh, God," Cory groaned in embarrassment. This was the very reason she didn't like wearing makeup. The black mascara was probably running down her cheeks in torrents. She felt like a fool and probably looked like something out of Michael Jackson's *Thriller* video, too.

"Thank you," she muttered quietly when she took it from his outstretched hand and started dabbing vigorously at her cheeks.

"Are you okay now, ma'am?" he asked, concerned.

Cory nodded. She was getting there at least.

"Good. Firstly allow me to apologize on behalf of the officers here for the utter disrespect directed at you by Officer Stewart. There was absolutely no need for him to be speaking to you in that manner, ma'am."

Shocked, Cory couldn't respond. Was this guy for real? Was he actually apologizing on behalf of the police? To a member of the public? Certainly, this had never happened to her before. Ever!

"And you might be?" Cory asked him. He must have a high rank or something, she thought.

"Well, as you could see, clearly I'm *not* a police officer." He smiled as he said this. "I'm second lieutenant Adrian Mendez. You know, ma'am, I wouldn't have liked to witness you being arrested out there just now."

"Arrested for what?" Cory cried out in utter amazement. "For standing up for my rights?"

"Actually, you looked like you were about to clobber Officer Stewart," he laughed. Cory was beginning to feel at ease with him. Strange enough, his words were warming to her. She felt comfortable. She felt comfortable and safe for the first time since she'd stepped foot in this Godforsaken place.

He continued, "Look, I'll be honest with you, ma'am. I really don't have a clue about taking stolen car reports."

"So why did you ask me to follow you, then?" Cory asked.

"You really looked like you needed some help."

Okay, so was second lieutenant a high rank? Cory wondered. Not that she really cared, but it sure sounded that way. And he certainly was very professional. Not to mention gorgeous. Cory was admiring the thick veins running through his folded hands as he crossed them against his wide chest. The way his military jacket fit snugly around his muscular arms. *Please look at the man's face, Cory,* she mentally warned herself.

But then again, he had the most unbelievably piercing eyes that followed her every move. Cory clutched her blouse at the opening. As if sensing her sudden discomfort, Adrian asked her about the make, color, and license plates of her vehicle. Cory gave him the details he asked her for. She noticed he wasn't writing anything down, either. So typical!

"Look, I already gave them all the information," Cory sighed.

"I know, Cory. But as Officer Stewart told you, the investigating officer, the one who took your initial report, Officer Franklin, isn't here right now. However, when he comes in I can find out what's the latest on your car for you. That's the most I can do at this point, I'm afraid."

"Well, I guess I have no choice, do I?" Cory muttered.

Diverting her gaze from his muscular body for the first time, Cory's eyes settled on the gray skies outside through the windows. Unbelievable! The sun had been shining a few minutes ago when she came in. Now, the clouds looked a menacing dark gray-black color, threatening to burst and unleash their fury over the city at any time. If it started raining, she didn't have an umbrella and she'd have to take a taxi back to her office.

"Oh, just great," Cory once again muttered to herself. She stood up and grabbed her handbag. "Well, if we're done here, I have to get back to work now."

Adrian stopped her. "Wait! Do you have a ride?"

"Oh yeah, but it was stolen, remember?" Cory shot back.

"So where're you heading? Maybe I could offer you a lift. I was on my way out, anyway," Adrian said. "If your boyfriend wouldn't mind."

Boyfriend? "Fortunately, I don't answer to anyone," Cory retorted.

"Well, I can't say I'm disappointed to hear that," Adrian said.

Though I'd love to ride you . . . . ride with you! What was wrong with her head? "No offense, but I really don't know you, okay," Cory coolly offered.

"But you know my name and rank. And where you could find me, too," Adrian said as he walked out with her.

"True. But that doesn't mean that I know you."

"I know. But I'll never allow any harm to come to you, Cory. Look, if anything happens to you once you're with me, you could always come back and report me," he added with a broad smile on his face.

Cory started laughing despite her foul mood.

"So you haven't answered me yet. Do you need that lift or not?" he pressed.

Cory realized the guy wasn't giving up. He seemed different

from the others. She knew she felt at ease with him. For someone so soft spoken, he had quite a commanding presence about him.

She stared at the sky again. The thick saturated clouds were heavy with rain, just waiting to burst. Cory knew all it took was a short but consistent shower to wreak havoc in this city. Flash flooding, heavy traffic jams, and stranded commuters were the resulting chaos.

Cory weighed her options. She could wait out the impending shower with Officer Stewart throwing comments left, right, and center or she take a taxi back to the office. Or, she could just accept the lift offered by this gorgeous soldier.

She looked at Adrian again. Then a sudden louder than usual crack of thunder rolled, causing Cory to nearly jump out of her skin. That sealed the deal. Maybe that thunder was a good sign, Cory reasoned. She knew she didn't want to stay here another second. "Okay, I'll go with you," she began hesitantly. She didn't want to come off as too desperate to him. Even if she was at the moment! "And only because it's going to rain and I don't have an umbrella with me right now."

Chapter 4

Cory followed him into the yard, trying her best to keep up with his long strides in her high heels. The rain started then, drizzling lightly at first but rapidly developing into bigger droplets. She heard an alarm deactivated and just in the nick of time, they reached his vehicle, a sleek black four-door pickup. It reminded Cory very much of the owner, muscular and rugged.

"Nice ride," she muttered under her breath as he opened the passenger door for her.

"Thanks."

Okay, so the guy could hear very well apparently. Cory hiked up her skirt hem a few inches to get into the monstrosity. Adrian's greedy eyes definitely took notice.

She sank into the plush richness of the luxurious crème-colored leather interior and buckled up. The interior gave off a heady masculine scent mixed in with the usual freshness of a new vehicle. This was a far cry from her car but she was nevertheless reminded of it.

Adrian turned on the AC and the radio. Soca music came blasting from the speakers. It was that time again on the island and one of Cory's favorites. Immediately after the festive Christmas holidays came the electrifying Carnival season, of which this type of music was an integral part. Soca was the modern, faster-paced version of the Calypso musical art form that had started way back during the time of slavery. Cory easily imagined slaves singing the songs to ease their pains and frustrations as they toiled all day long in the sugar-cane fields. Maybe she should start singing Calypso, she thought.

A thick, white rain was pouring heavily now. Traffic was at a crawl, as she'd expected. When it rained, everyone drove slower just to be safe. Well, at least she had eye candy.

The temperature inside cooled down pretty quickly but why

was she still feeling the heat? This stranger's body next to hers was radiating such warmth. Or was it all in her vivid imagination?

Cory couldn't help but suppress a smile when she noticed the strong intent plastered on Adrian's face as he fought to keep his focus on driving through the heavy rain instead of on her bare flashing legs she deliberately left exposed. She had caught him outright staring and the poor guy was having such a hard time concentrating now. Jay would be so proud of her!

*

Adrian drove through the rain, he tried to concentrate on maneuvering his vehicle safely through the water-filled streets. He certainly couldn't afford to be distracted. He certainly didn't need an accident, either. What was he going to say? It was all her fault. Exposing her luscious legs like that for him to stare at. He didn't mean to stare but all she had to do was pull the damn hem of her skirt down a little, instead of tempting him out of his damn mind. Adrian doubted this would do him any good, though. The damage was already done. He'd already seen them and they would forever be ingrained in his head. Just like all her other well-defined body parts.

But he was practically sweating in the AC. In fact, nothing would please him more than taming the flame of desire burning in him. Adrian mentally scolded himself for losing his concentration like that, especially when he was driving. But all his thoughts apparently became incoherent since butting in to protect this woman. It really wasn't his fault. He was a mere hot-blooded male, after all . . . with needs. And which living man on this earth wouldn't be enticed by this fiery, sun-kissed island goddess just a mere touch away from him?

Finally, breaking the uncomfortable silence growing between them, Adrian asked, "So do you really understand Spanish?"

"Yes. I'm bilingual."

"Well, I think that's truly amazing. Imagine, my father came from a Spanish heritage and I can't even speak the language. And I never even thought for a second that I would've ended up in the motherland either."

"You've been to Spain?"

"Yes."

"How did you end up there?"

"A couple years back, when I was a Marine, I went on a maritime security operations tour to the Mediterranean and Persian Gulf." He had spent seven months at sea on board a U.S. carrier during that particular deployment. Probably his best tour ever, making port visits and ensuring security cooperation in not only Spain but in Greece, Turkey, Bahrain, and the United Arab Emirates.

"Wait a minute, *you* were a *U.S. Marine*?" Cory asked, in a perplexed tone.

"Yep."

"So aren't you guys supposed to be natural-born killers?" she asked, a worried look now spreading on her face.

Adrian chuckled at her question. He didn't see himself as one but decided to go along anyway. "Well, sort of. Depending how you look at it." Marines had mastered amphibious warfare techniques, raid techniques, scouting, patrolling, weapons recognition, airborne, surface and sub-surface insertion and extraction techniques and free-fall parachuting. All were a part of their training to kill.

Instantly sensing her discomfort, Adrian tried reassuring her. "You can relax, Cory. The average person thinks the U.S. armed forces only fight wars in the Middle East. But we do undertake humanitarian and goodwill missions around the world. We don't only repel enemy assault fire." He flashed a smile.

"Oh, I know all what your job entails," Cory retorted.

"You do?" Adrian shot her a surprised look.

"Let's just say, I follow the wars from *unbiased* sources."

"Ah, an informed civilian," he couldn't help but remark. "I'm impressed."

"My job requires me to pay attention to international affairs," she said. "Anything that could have an impact on the oil price. The worldwide economic downturn, natural disasters, strikes and industrial action, and the wars in the Middle East."

Brains and beauty, Adrian thought.

"So did you serve in a war zone?" she asked.

"In Afghanistan," Adrian answered. "Kabul."

"And how was it over there?"

"Let's just say, I'm extremely happy to be here," Adrian laughed. He didn't feel the need to bore her with the gory details.

"That bad, huh? I suppose you had your hands full repelling enemy fire," she offered with slight disdain in her voice.

"Excuse me?" Adrian didn't know how else to respond to that. "That's what happens in a war."

"I'm sure. And even civilian casualties?"

"Unfortunately, that happens, too," Adrian answered slowly. "Sometimes."

"Well, I think it's terribly wrong when innocent bystanders are the ones who get killed." She was getting angry.

"Look, Cory, I certainly didn't make the rules of combat. There have been wars long before my time and there'll be wars long after," Adrian added in an even tone. "I'm sensing some animosity here. Do you have family serving or something?"

"Of course not!" Cory blurted out. "So why're you *here*, then? Tired of shooting people?"

"Something like that," Adrian answered grimly.

"So why did you leave your rodme?" Cory demanded.

"I didn't leave my home," Adrian shot back. "I *am* home."

"Oh, really? Well, that American accent isn't fooling anybody. You certainly don't sound like us, by the way," Cory huffed.

"Really?"

"Uh-huh."

"Well, you can't blame a guy for trying," he laughed out loud then. Adrian saw a smile and Cory wore it beautifully on that gorgeous face of hers. "Actually, I was born here, Cory."

Adrian was accustomed to this. Almost everywhere he went on the island people always asked him if he was an American citizen. The truth was, he was both. Although sharing a Trini-American heritage did have its many perks, for him, the best part about it, together with the shared citizenship was that he was able to serve both great countries. A fact he was proud of. Not too many people were afforded this rare privilege. He explained his story to Cory.

If his father hadn't suffered such a tragic death, Adrian knew he would have grown up on the island. His life would have turned out quite differently all together. His father had been a major in the army when he was killed. Adrian was only nine, but that was a day he would never forget for as long as he lived. Adrian remembered hearing the blast from where he was playing in the yard. They had lived not too far from the army base, in St. James. He had no idea that it had something to do with his father until the soldiers came by to tell his mother the bad news.

It was a story he had heard numerous times as a child growing up. His father was waiting in a military jeep getting ready to come home when there was an explosion caused by a bush fire or something at the camp where he was based. Several other soldiers were also killed and many were injured as a result of the blast. Adrian remembered this clearly because his father had promised to take him and Anna for pizza that evening. But they never got any. Only their mother's anguished screams filled them that evening.

His father's death robbed him of barefoot childhood days, climbing mango trees with his cousins and racing bicycles down the potholed neighborhood streets. His mother couldn't cope with his father's death, so she took her two young children and fled to the comforts of her homeland in the U.S.

"So to be politically correct, I guess that makes you an African-American-Hispanic-Trinidadian, then," Cory offered.

"Something like that," Adrian grinned at her assessment.

"Interesting. So what brought you back, then?"

"I love the place. Trinidad's pretty much like the Big Apple for me." The land of his birth was equally as vibrant and diversely multicultural but still very much a tropical island paradise to him. "And I guess you could say I couldn't resist the charms of the beautiful women here at the same time," he added, looking Cory dead in her eyes.

His mother always insisted he got his incredible good looks and mannerisms from his father, from his light brown skin tone to his charm. It was this charm Adrian was trying his hardest to work now.

Seeing Cory blush profusely, Adrian figured it was actually working. "I just have to ask you this . . . why'd you buy that car, anyway?"

"Because it was at a really good price," Cory answered quite frankly. "Not everyone can afford something like this," she mumbled under her breath.

Ignoring her last comment, Adrian asked, "Didn't you know that's the number one car of choice for jackings here?"

"No, I didn't know that," Cory answered.

"Don't you read the newspapers or listen to the news?"

"Local news? I don't actually," Cory indignantly shot back.

"Well, that figures," Adrian muttered.

"So let me guess, this is a police statistic, right?"

"Yes. It is actually."

"I guess you learn something new every day," she said. "And by the way, just in case you're wondering, I'm heading around the Savannah."

"Oh, right. I forgot to ask you that." It was just that he could have driven around the island and back once he had that amazing view of her luscious flesh. Not that he was complaining or anything. There was a perfect pair of smooth brown legs for his eyes to enjoy. The problem, however, was his eyes alone weren't enjoying the view. Adrian was imagining what they would feel like against his touch or those well-defined legs wrapped around his waist right about now when his delicious thoughts were interrupted by Cory's voice. She was telling him the name of the street she was dropping off at.

"So then may I presume from all your bitter sentiments about military men that it all stems from a bad relationship with one of them?" he asked.

"I didn't have a bad relationship," Cory said. "But I know way too many women who have. No offense but you guys aren't exactly my type."

Adrian was almost positive he knew her type. "And why is that?" He couldn't wait to hear her answer to this one.

"Why is what?"

"Why do the women here think the worst of us?"

"Oh, that's easy. First, let's see," Cory began counting on her fingers. "You all usually have the tendency to stray and cheat. You lie. You all tend to be abusive, too. That military uniform signifies that you're all just dogs, plain and simple."

Adrian knew all about the stigma associated with the military men on the island. They were usually regarded as womanizers. But this lady was extremely harsh in her assessment.

"Whoa, I'm just really sorry I asked you that question now." Adrian laughed despite himself. "But I'm a soldier and I don't think I'm abusive or a dog or anything like that."

"Well, good for you."

"As much as you dislike the military, you seem to dislike the police even more." He thought about her doing battle with Officer Stewart.

"I have good reasons to," Cory didn't hesitate to respond.

"Like what?"

"Just trust me, I have a lot of reasons, okay."

Adrian just left it at that. He realized Cory probably didn't want to divulge those reasons to a perfect stranger, especially one who worked with them.

"They just don't do their damn jobs," Cory blurted after a while.

"C'mon, not all of them are like that," Adrian said.

"That's because they're your friends," Cory shot back at him.

"Not all of them are. Look, there're some really hardworking and professional officers out there," Adrian countered. "Stewart, unfortunately, isn't one of them."

"Yeah? Well name one who is!" Cory demanded.

There were several of them Adrian could have named. Those who executed their duties diligently and served their country with pride. A close friend of his, Sergeant Jones, who was stationed right where they were. Then there was his aunt, now an inspector. She was definitely a woman of steel.

There were also the officers he worked with in his unit. They were the best of the bunch definitely and he trusted them with his life. And that was one thing he was indeed grateful for, his own life. In this line of work, living to see another day had become Adrian's personal mantra. One false move and it could be your last day on earth. It was a U.S. Marine's rule to never leave a man behind. The same could be said for here. Watching out for each other's back was an understood pact with everyone in his unit.

"All I'm saying is that you shouldn't class all of us in the same light, especially when using someone like Stewart, of all people, as the measuring stick. Because that's just plain stereotyping in my book," Adrian ended quietly.

When Cory remained silent, Adrian figured she was trying her best to ignore him, so he continued. "You know, we could also do some stereotyping of our own, too." She shot him a nasty look but still didn't say anything so again he took the liberty to go on and prove his point. "For instance, from our observations we could say that women like you are pampered princesses spoiled rotten by your rich daddies and most likely use what the Almighty blessed you with to get whatever you want."

"*What?*" Cory's head snapped up. "Excuse me, but I work extremely hard for whatever I want . . . just so you know that. How dare you insinuate that I use my body to get my way? And what the hell do you know about my father, anyway? And for your information, Mr. Ex-Marine-Sir, I have a *master's degree* so I certainly don't need to use my body for anything other than pleasure, when *I* feel like it."

And Adrian would certainly love to help her do just that. Now, preferably. "There's no such thing as an ex-Marine. Once a Marine. Always a Marine," was his response instead. Adrian couldn't help it. He had to laugh at the incredulous look now plastered on Cory's face. She, however, clearly wasn't in a joking mood.

"You were pretty quick to take offense. Well, I'm truly sorry if I offended you, Cory, but I wasn't really referring to you in particular, just so you understand that. Now you probably realize how military personnel feel. We're not all the same." After all, he was in the military and he wasn't a player, neither was he an abuser. How could he ever be abusive to any woman when the only people in his life *were* women? "So I guess the lesson learned here is that we all shouldn't be stereotyping one another."

"Whatever!" Cory spat back at him. "You know what? I think you need to drop me off here, please."

"But this isn't the street you told me."

"I know. I guess I changed my mind."

"Look . . . it's still raining," Adrian pointed at the window with his free hand.

"That's okay, it's just a drizzle now. I'm sure I won't melt. Right here is perfect."

Adrian put on his indicator to pull to the left on the wet and slippery road and cautiously pulled over.

"Thank you," Cory said. When the vehicle finally came to a stop, she practically ran out, ensuring she slammed the door good and hard in the process.

Adrian jumped when it slammed in his face. "What the hell . . . ." he murmured. She didn't look like she had all that strength in her. He must have really pissed her off.

*

Cory was royally pissed off for the second time today. This was all she needed, another man trying to tell her what to do. She had a father, a younger brother, and a boss who apparently had a stick up his ass all going neck-to-neck already. She knew by the time she reached the office, she would be completely soaked. This didn't faze her either, as mad as hell as she was.

Cory now had to walk an entire block to her office building. At this point, she didn't really care. She was cold and hungry but mostly relieved Adrian didn't get to see where she actually worked. Just in case he had any stalker-tendencies up his military repertoire.

Now would have certainly been a good time to have her car, she fumed. If only some officers would just do their damn jobs every once in a while. And how dare Adrian Mendez defend their inefficiencies? So typical these men in uniform, they always banded together.

Chapter 5

Adrian wasn't a happy camper when Cory fled his vehicle but he knew better than to go against a woman's wishes. Still a bit stunned, he wondered how a great, stimulating conversation could have taken such a drastic turn for the worst in just a few minutes. *When you opened your big mouth and insinuated that the lady was a ho, that's when,* he scolded himself.

"Shit!" Why on earth would he say something so disrespectful like that to her? Never in his lifetime had a woman ever fled from his presence or slammed a door so hard in his face before. "You really worked that charm, Mendez," Adrian chided himself.

He remained parked and watched Cory saunter down the street. He admired her skill to walk in those heels and still possess the ability to make him drool. Even in the drizzle and from behind, Adrian got the message loud and clear just how much of a sexy woman Cory was. He silently watched her until she disappeared around the corner.

He figured he knew exactly where she was heading. For someone who spoke fluent Spanish and dropped off around this area, there were two clear choices. Either it was one of those Latin American embassies or the Spanish oil multinational.

Adrian went with his gut feeling that it was the oil company she was heading to, since she kept her eyes on the oil price and she did look like more of the serious businesswoman type, in those power suits and high heels. But if he was right, this was just two buildings down on the corner. So why was she walking all the way down another street? Probably to throw him off, he figured. He guessed then Miss-Want-to-Walk-in-the-Rain underestimated his military skills. Being observant and paying attention to details were major requirements.

As Adrian drove away, his mind was telling him to just leave it for what it was, a mere chance encounter, but an incongruous, exciting feeling was coursing through him. Strange, because it felt like an entire lifetime ago since he was this much excited by the opposite sex. Adrian had only spent a short time with Cory and already she evoked in him all these things, excitement, sensuality, lust.

Clearly, something about her had captivated him. Was it the hair, her beautiful eyes, her scent? Maybe it was the way her brain worked? Or maybe it was that damn feistiness in her today. Those sexy legs sure would do the trick, too. But this woman most definitely had issues. But too bad, he was already hooked. And he needed to see her again.

*

It was already after six in the evening when Adrian finally finished his training session for the day. He was getting ready to leave but first made a stop by his good friend's office before heading out. Forget about Franklin, he was starting at the top. Adrian knew Jonesie was one of the few policemen he could trust at this particular station. And one who would help him with anything.

"Aye, Jonesie, what's going on, man?"

"Mendez, I heard you were looking for me," bellowed Sergeant Jones in his lovely island accent. Jones was a friendly looking police officer in his early forties. He and Adrian got along very well and they had been friends ever since he started training the guys here.

Adrian entered Jonesie's office and said, "Yes. I wanted to find out something and you're the only man here who can help me."

"And what's that exactly?"

Adrian wasted no time. "Early New Year's morning, a young lady came in here to report her car stolen."

"You have to do better than that, Mendez. There were about three stolen cars that night. So tell me which one exactly."

Adrian told him. "The woman's name is Cory Phillips."

Jones flipped through some papers on his desk and then

answered, "Yes. Why didn't you just say that? Miss Head Turner. Getting every man in here confused in that dress she was wearing. Even you, Mendez," Jonesie added, laughing.

"Me?"

"Yeah. I saw you looking. You couldn't take your eyes off her."

Adrian grinned. He didn't think anyone would have noticed him staring. "But could you really blame me?" Not only was Cory a naturally stunning woman, she exuded immense sexuality. Add in intelligence and confidence and these characteristics alone made women appear even sexier in Adrian's book. "Anyway, I had to intervene on her behalf with Stewart today."

"Yeah, I heard about that."

"And you know that I'd never question your men in the line of carrying out their duties, right?"

"Yes, I know that, Mendez."

"Not that I really give a shit about Stewart anyway but the guy was completely way out of line today. You need to talk to him, Jonesie."

"Mendez, I can't tell you how many times I've spoken to Stewart about his behavior. I get a lot of complaints from the public about him."

"No wonder."

"Yeah. Don't worry over it. I'll take care of him. So why and what do you need to find out?"

"Well, I sort of had an interesting conversation with her today and I sort of promised her that I'd try to see what I could find out about her car." Adrian smiled.

"Mendez boy, why did you have to go and promise that woman the impossible? Haven't I taught you nothin' my friend?" Jones erupted but both men laughed heartily.

"So Jonesie, you know you have to find that car, right?"

"Oh. I see where this is going now," Jonesie laughed. "You're trying to get *lucky*, my friend."

"I don't know what you're talking about, man," Adrian said. "I'm merely trying to help a young lady in distress. And on top of which, she really hates policemen."

"And she likes soldiers I presume?" Jones asked dryly.

"Negative. She dislikes us all in uniform. Look, she really needs her car back, man."

"Yeah, Mendez, you just keep telling yourself that," Jonesie said knowingly.

"So what's the status on it, anyway?"

"There's an All-Points-Bulletin in all the divisions but so far, no sightings of it anywhere."

"Well, please try to push this one through for me."

"I'll try."

"Thanks, man. I knew I could count on you. And Jonesie, please make everything as quick and comfortable for her the next time she comes back here."

"Will do, Mendez. But if we find it, the rest is up to you, son," he chuckled. Heading out the door now, Adrian stopped, "Oh yeah, one more thing, Jonesie. Please keep Stewart the hell away from her."

This time, Adrian was very serious.

"No problem. So you'll let me know if you get through, right?" Jones continued chuckling in his office.

It had been another long and grueling day for Adrian but it wasn't over yet. Back in his vehicle, Adrian was now headed for base to finish up some paperwork there. It would be another all-nighter behind his desk because he wasn't getting off till eight the next morning. Yet, he still had to love his job.

Adrian really hoped Jonesie would pull through on this favor for him though. He definitely needed to see Cory again. Although he was pretty confident he knew exactly where he could find her.

Chapter 6

By the time an infuriated and completely drenched Cory had reached her office, she knew she hated the police more than ever. She hated the rain more than ever. And she couldn't stop thinking about second lieutenant Adrian Mendez.

She was exhausted. She felt like she had just fought a war with her near fracas at the station. She felt battered and abused. Not physically, but her ego had taken a brutal beat down today. The only good thing that probably came out from all this was the lift she was offered by Adrian. Or was that such a good thing?

Although she didn't really bank on his promise to look into the matter for her, nevertheless Cory still hoped. She needed to deal with the insurance company and bank next. This was going to be an all-out war but she wasn't scared. She never backed down from a battle. Her sharp tongue and quick wit always got her out of tough situations.

Thoughts of Adrian filled her head all afternoon. She still didn't know why she acted like such a fool and darted out of the man's vehicle. He was only trying for her to see his point, after all. Cory felt like something had really clicked between them though. She blushed as she remembered her body being completed turned on by him. She was curious to find out what else he was capable of doing to her.

Maybe she needed a man like Adrian to help her relieve some of life's stresses, she pondered. She hadn't noticed a ring on his finger. Then again, the military men on this island always secretly or otherwise wore more than one woman on their arms at any given time.

Still, Cory couldn't remember the last time any man had her this much flustered.

Precisely three days after her encounter with Adrian, Cory received a telephone call from a Sergeant Jones while finishing a quick lunch in her office.

"Ma'am, I have some good news for you."

"And what's that exactly?" Cory started to feel hopeful.

"We found your car."

"Really? Where?" asked a now-excited Cory.

"In Guanapo."

Guanapo? From Cory's quick geographic recollection of the island, Guanapo was a tiny but heavily forested village in the east. "Is it still in one piece?" she asked just to make sure.

"Yes, ma'am, it is."

"Excellent! So when can I come for my car?" she asked. Cory was wasting no more time with this. Not having her car for almost a week now was killing her physically and mentally.

"Well, it has to go to forensics to get checked out."

"Forensics? Why?"

"That's just standard procedure to see if anything was tampered with in the vehicle."

"Okay."

"Well, how about I give you a call by Thursday, then."

"Sounds great. Thanks, Sergeant," and Cory ended the call.

"Yessss!" she screamed ecstatically in the confines of her office and swiveled merrily in her chair. It was only when she got up to do a little erotic gyration of her hips did Cory notice her boss standing in the doorway.

"Is everything okay in here?" Javier enquired in his sexy Spanish accent—the only thing he had going for him, apparently.

"Everything is fine," a caught off-guard Cory quickly responded.

"Good. I need this back by three." Javier proceeded to drop a stack of visibility reports on her desk before making a quick exit.

"Idiot," Cory muttered under her breath once he was safely out of earshot. But not even Javier could spoil her mood right now. She couldn't believe it. The police had finally done their jobs after all. And all it took were a little melodrama, her acting all gangsta, screaming her head off, and shedding a few tears in the process.

But that was beside the point now, she was thankful to be getting her car back.

Cory couldn't help but wonder if Adrian had anything to do with this. He had promised that he'd look into it for her. Not that she was really expecting him to do anything. Why would he, anyway? Certainly not after the way she had acted and rudely bolted the other day. She had wanted to ask Sergeant Jones this but held her tongue after thinking that it might seem inappropriate. Cory immediately called Jay to tell him the good news.

*

Sure enough, when Thursday finally came around Sergeant Jones called and insisted she ask for him directly when she arrived. After what had transpired the last time, Cory wasn't taking any chances. She didn't want a repeat, so she asked Jay to remain with her.

They walked into the station a little after noon and she was in a really good mood—up until she spotted Stewart intently staring her down. This time, he didn't say a word to her. Cory was thankful he didn't because she would have definitely gotten arrested today. Instead, she walked up to a female officer and asked for Sergeant Jones.

She couldn't believe the swiftness with which they were all moving today. It was like a totally new police force altogether. Right away she and Jay were led to Sergeant Jones's office. When she entered, she was met by a very jovial man.

"Ah, Miss Phillips. Come in, come in," he said with a smile, ushering her in with a handshake and giving Jay a pleasant nod. Cory couldn't believe she was receiving all this royal treatment.

Her wardrobe was carefully chosen as was her norm, but for today, it was extra-special, just in case she ran into a particular second lieutenant again. She had looked a bit of a frazzled disaster when Adrian had given her a lift last time. She didn't want a repeat of that fiasco, either.

She was wearing a burnt orange blouse with a plunging neckline. This was neatly tucked into her slim brown pencil skirt ending above her knees. Her outfit was complemented by four-inch brown pumps. Her attention-grabbing ensemble definitely accentuated her vivacious curves, from her full bosom to her tiny waist, wide hips, and shapely calves.

Sergeant Jones spoke to her briefly before leading her and Jay outside. They headed over to where her car was. Cory breathed a sigh of relief when she saw that it really was in a good condition still. When she was told that she was free to go with it, only then did Jay leave.

This went well, Cory breathed. She had only spent about fifteen minutes in total here. A world record, perhaps? As she started her car, Cory mustered enough courage to ask Jones, "By the way, is Second Lieutenant Mendez around?"

"No, my dear," Jones replied. "Mendez isn't based here."

"Oh." Cory felt disappointed when she heard this. It probably showed all over her face because Jones said, with a hint of mischief in his voice, "He's over at the base."

Cory didn't know what the mischief was all about—all she wanted was to find Adrian and apologize. "So where exactly is this base located?"

Chapter 7

Sergeant Jones's directions proved to be quite good. Cory was able to find the base in uptown Port of Spain without any trouble. She'd never realized it existed even though she had passed there numerous times before. She also couldn't believe that it was within close proximity to her own office. As she pulled into the military compound, the young, good-looking soldier manning the gateway immediately stopped her vehicle. Cory automatically rolled down the passenger window so she could speak to him.

"Good afternoon, ma'am," the soldier said.

"Good afternoon, I'm here to see Second Lieutenant Adrian Mendez," Cory announced.

"He isn't here right now, ma'am."

"Will he be here soon?" she asked hopefully.

"He usually is. If no emergencies come up."

"Okay, well, can I take the chance and wait for him, then?"

"Sure, ma'am. You can wait over there if you like," the soldier said, pointing with his hand to a parking area behind him.

"Thanks." Cory ended the conversation and sent the window up again. She drove toward the car park that gleamed like a magnificent black animal from the scorching midday sun overhead. Cory noticed Adrian's pickup and her mind immediately flashed to his sexy smile and that was enough to send her temperature soaring.

For now, she sat in the car and waited, amazed and thankful that all the car's accessories were still in place—especially the AC. It kept her body cool. Cory knew one look at Adrian in the flesh and her body temperature might skyrocket to boiling point this time. It had happened to her twice. She nervously wondered if it would happen a third time.

As the minutes ticked by, her anticipation to see him again built. She felt excited, like a young school girl.

What if he didn't want to see her? Well, it would serve her right. She hadn't been exactly polite to the man after he was kind enough to offer her a lift in the first place. She'd practically bolted from him, as if he had attacked her or something, preferring to walk in the rain instead.

If only she could turn back the hands of time, she would have been a lot more courteous and gracious. This was the main reason she was here now, Cory reminded herself. She wanted to say a personal thank you to Adrian for all his help. She also needed to apologize for her very rude behavior the other day. But she was becoming more nervous by the minute. Was she ready to do this now?

"What the hell am I doing here?" Cory asked herself out aloud.

*

Adrian was sitting in the front passenger's seat when he pulled into the base with the other soldiers and officers. The sentry on duty stopped them and came directly to him.

"LT, there's someone here waiting to see you, sir."

"Who?" Adrian asked, surprised.

"A young lady, sir. She's in the car park waiting," the soldier told him.

Strange. Adrian was wondering who his visitor could be amidst the snickering of the others. The only female he allowed to visit him here was his sister and usually she called him first.

Just as the driver started moving again, out of nowhere a car swung directly onto their path, braking mere inches in front of them. His driver had to slam on his brakes to avoid a head-on collision.

*

"Oh my God," Cory screamed, clutching her chest. She'd hit her breaks so hard just now she swore all her curls would bounce right off her head. That was when she saw him. Her heart nearly gave way. Butterflies did a dance in her stomach. Adrian alighted from his vehicle and began walking toward her. Cory was breathing heavily. She didn't know if it was from her near-death experience just now or from the sight of him approaching. She had to get it together. Fast.

Cory stared, her foot still mashing down hard on the brakes. It was her first time seeing him in full military gear. He struck a striking picture, from the beret on his head to the boots on his feet. Tall, handsome, professional, authoritative, strong and powerful—dangerous, even. A black bullet-proof vest was strapped across his broad chest and dark-green camouflage fatigues, his strong veined hand nestled firmly on the huge gun in front him.

Cory didn't understand why at this particular moment she was so unbelievably happy to see him. Nor had she expected her reaction at seeing him again to be so lustful. And to think she had almost missed all this luscious manliness by choosing to leave in such a hurry. Maybe because she nearly died just now, Cory found him to be highly irresistible. What was it about this particular soldier that she found so damn sexy in that uniform?

*

As Adrian bent and tapped on the window of the nutcase who was driving the car, he saw crazy curls spilling everywhere. So *she* was his visitor? He couldn't believe she was actually here in the flesh. No, he was more like shocked, but Adrian was so glad Cory Phillips almost crashed into him. What was she doing here? The last time he saw her, she all but ran away from him. And she had been on his mind since.

After getting a more-than-generous glimpse of those gorgeous legs of hers, he'd had some dreams about her. Most of them, he had to admit, were of an erotic nature. Hey, if he couldn't have her in real life, at least he could have her in his dreams. There weren't any rules against that, right? Adrian smiled at his erotic thoughts as he tapped her window again and she slowly let it down.

"Are you trying to get yourself killed, ma'am?" Adrian smiled down at her. The last time he'd seen her, she was so angry and sad. Well, this was no sad, crying woman but a rather happy one smiling back at him. He liked this new found cheerfulness in her. It suited her much better.

"Hi," she flashed a sexy smile.

"Cory, what a nice surprise," Adrian offered in return. He wasn't lying. She was the last person on this earth he had expected to see here, today or ever.

Adrian forgot all about his men waiting in the vehicle. The driver honking on the horn brought his attention back to them. "Go around, man!" Adrian shouted at him.

"Oh, I'm soooo sorry about this," Cory apologized.

"Don't worry about it. Nobody got hurt. Especially you," Adrian offered. "So I see you got your car back . . . finally."

"Yeah, I just did. I asked Sergeant Jones where I could find you. I hope you don't mind?"

Mind? Was she kidding? Adrian thought. She was the perfect distraction. "Well, I'm really happy for you, Cory. So . . . what do I owe the pleasure of this visit?"

"Umm, I just stopped by because I wanted to say thank you for all your help."

"So what makes you think I had anything to do with this?" Adrian asked, still smiling sweetly at her.

"Well, for one, I think I received the royal treatment from your friends today." They both laughed. Adrian believed her; he had asked Jonesie to warn his men to be nice.

Adrian walked to the back of the car, inspecting it. He had to preoccupy his mind with something, anything, other than being enticed by her heaving cleavage, a sight he was enjoying a bit too much.

"You need to get a new tail light, okay," he said. "Other than that, I think you're in pretty good shape. You're a lucky woman, you know. Thieves usually scrap these as soon as they steal them. They probably just used yours for a robbery."

"Well, I guess I am lucky." Hesitating a bit, Cory continued, "Well, I also wanted to apologize to you for my very rude behavior the other day, Adrian."

"Hey, everyone has their bad days. And no offense was taken," Adrian assured her.

"Really? Well, please allow me to make it up to you, then. What're you doing this evening?"

"Working."

"Oh. So what time do you get off?"

"At eight. Tomorrow morning," Adrian quickly added.

"*What?*"

"Yeah. We work twenty-four-hour shifts here."

"My God, how do you work all day and then stay up all night, too?" Cory asked.

"Well, you get used to it after a while."

"Okay. Well, I was about to ask you out to have some drinks with me. To show my appreciation and to apologize and everything. My treat, of course."

Adrian was amused. "You don't have to do that," he said. "I have to shoulder part of the blame myself with some of the things I said to you."

A look of disappointment crossed her face. *She wanted to go out with him?* "But let me get this straight. You're asking me out?" Adrian was smiling again. "Seriously though?"

"Yes!" Cory answered. "You sound surprised. Has a woman never offered to buy you drinks before?"

"Never," Adrian answered her with a grin. The women he dated in the past were more like friends of his friends or friends of his cousins and the like. Most were okay, but nothing he wanted to pursue. Some turned literally into the dates from hell where all he wanted to do was dive through the closest window to make an escape from them.

But he'd always done the asking, so he was stunned stunned at Cory's brazen invitation. Adrian knew he didn't have a fighting chance with this woman, with her perfectly manicured nails and power suits. He figured he wasn't her type. He was just a soldier in her book. Though a financially secure, educated, and well-traveled one at that. After all, she had made her feelings quite clear the way she felt about men like him the other day.

But the mere thought of Cory and he got excited. She stimulated his senses in every way. From her skin that smelled—and he imagined felt—like a floral bouquet, to her crazy hair, her smile, her sexy feminine saunter, those damn legs she often left exposed.

"Never? I find that hard to believe."

Looking her dead in her eyes Adrian said, "But I'm always willing to try something new."

Adrian lived his life taking huge risks in combat zones and overcoming challenges every day. Why should he hesitate to take up this one? Actually, this was one challenge he was looking forward to taking.

"So how about we do this tomorrow evening instead?" Adrian suggested.

"That's perfect," Cory replied. She gave him the name of the sports bar and the time to meet her at.

"Cory, why don't you join me in my office for a while? It's so hot out here," Adrian offered. "I was about to have lunch."

Cory quickly accepted his offer this time.

Chapter 8

As they walked together toward Adrian's office, Cory found herself once again trying to keep up with his long strides. She noticed he had a methodical rhythm when he walked. As they neared the small green military buildings, the base was pretty much quiet and didn't have as much activity as Cory had expected there.

"Do you mind waiting here a minute?" Adrian asked her. "I'll be right back."

"Sure."

Adrian immediately took off and disappeared into another room. Cory remained standing there, alone. She noticed she was receiving quite a few unwanted stares from some officers passing by. These two looked quite intimidating in their black and blue uniforms, their black boots and weapons gleaming under the sun's intense rays.

She was relieved to see Adrian heading back her way, nodding at the two policemen. He was holding a set of dangling keys in his hands along with two bottles of water perched on top a white polystyrene container Cory presumed was his lunch.

"Sorry 'bout that," he apologized, unlocking a door close by. He entered the room and motioned for Cory to step inside. He turned on the air-conditioning with the remote and proceeded to close the door behind her. "Welcome to my humble office," he announced.

Humble was right. Cory looked around and there wasn't much of anything there at all. The room was small, hot, and stuffy. There were only two desks and two chairs with a computer monitor and keyboard perched on top of one of them. Definitely, Adrian's office was nothing like the ones she was accustomed to. The ones in her building were big, bright, and tastefully decorated. Not to mention they had a million dollar view of the Queen's Park Savannah. One of the main reasons for the ridiculous real estate prices for property in that area.

Cory watched a bit apprehensively as Adrian removed his gun. He seemed to sense her discomfort because he said, "Don't worry, it won't just go off."

"I just don't like guns. At all. They scare me," she admitted. "This is the first time I've seen one up close."

He nodded and put the weapon on the other desk, as far from Cory as possible. Great, now she could concentrate on him and what he was saying without feeling like she could be shot at any moment. Next, he unsnapped and removed his bullet-proof vest. Adrian then took the liberty of removing his military jacket and was sensitive enough to drape it over his gun, totally obscuring it from Cory's view. The man was stripping in front of her, revealing his snug-fitting T-shirt underneath. Cory wondered why he even found it necessary to wear it in the first place. She was expecting to see some of that honeyed skin below. Well, if he was bold enough to be ogling her, she sure as hell could ogle him back!

After opening a bottle of water, Adrian offered it to her. As soon as he opened his, he took a long gulp, finishing the bottle in another go. Cory watched him as he took the water in his mouth, the movement of his jaw as it went down his throat. She needed a sip herself just from looking at him do that.

"That was good," Adrian said as he tossed the empty bottle in the bin. The tropical heat was overwhelming today. It felt like another blistering 97 degrees and the nearby sea offered no comforting cool breezes over the land mass. On this island, when the sun shone, it really did, beating down on the islanders like a slave being mercilessly whipped by his master. Then, when it rained, it poured. This was the typical tropical weather pattern in the Caribbean.

"I guess you're not as hot as I am," Adrian innocently commented after looking at Cory's three-quarter filled bottle of water.

Oh, the mischievous thoughts that were going on in her head in response to that shocked even her.

Cory looked around and didn't notice any photos on his desk or on the walls. No paintings or plants even. Just bare walls and starkness. Rather, the only thing in Adrian's office of interest to her was a huge map on his desk.

"Hey, is this a map of the city?" Cory asked. She leaned over and closely scrutinized the huge map that practically filled Adrian's desk.

"Yes, it is," he answered.

"And this is only of the capital?" she asked again with the inquisitiveness of a child.

"Yeah, it's a very detailed one actually," Adrian answered looking quite amused. "It's to help us with our patrols in the city."

"I should get one of these for my office wall." Cory scoured the map for her own office location.

"Why don't you come over here? You'll see it much better right side up," Adrian joked.

He motioned for Cory to join him on the other side of the small desk and she obliged, quickly scooting across. "Show me where we are," Cory said.

Adrian covered her right hand with his and used both their index fingers to point to a spot on the map.

"Here we are," he whispered in that low, sexy voice Cory was beginning to love.

At that exact moment, they could have been in Timbuktu for all she cared. She couldn't concentrate on anything besides the warmth of Adrian's body slowly seeping through hers, his strong hand covering hers, and his hot breath in her ear. Her knees were getting weaker with every second. Cory grabbed on to the desk with her other hand fearing she would faint or something. The sexual tension between them was unmistakably flaring.

Cory caught her breath as Adrian slowly turned her body to meet his, holding her firmly but gently with his other hand.

Cory pressed her soft curves up against his rock-hard body as

Adrian pulled her even closer. There was a smoldering look in his eyes as he lowered his head to kiss her. The anticipation was too intense as Cory waited for his hot lips to brush hers for the very first time. Without disappointing, Adrian kissed her slowly, softly.

His warm hand caressed her neck causing her to inhale sharply. *Breathe stupid, breathe,* Cory thought. As Adrian's lips brushed hers, a sweetness and warmth flowed all the way down to her toes. When she responded to him with the same eagerness and intensity, both their passions ignited.

Cory closed her eyes. After what seemed like sweet eternity, Adrian hesitantly raised his lips from hers. Cory didn't want this kiss to end.

"Thank you for not slapping me, Cory, but honestly, I wanted to do that since the first time I saw you," he admitted.

Fresh shivers ricocheted throughout her body with his admission. "Why would I ever want to slap you?"

Adrian smiled and kissed her again, more fiercely this time. As his tongue slipped inside her mouth, Cory moaned.

He lifted his head. "Shhh," he whispered in her ear and placed his index finger gently against her lips. "Easy, baby."

"Sorry," she giggled softly. "I'm just loving this." Cory took his same finger and kissed it. Then, a naughty grin flashed across her face, she slowly inserted it into her mouth. She playfully sucked on it.

"Are you enjoying teasing me, Cory?" Adrian asked in a raspy voice, laced thick with sensual passion.

"Uh-huh." She didn't know what had come over her just now. Suddenly, she felt so alive, so uninhibited. So brave and wanton, all wrapped in one horny package.

"Well, then I have to warn you," Adrian began, kissing her along her neck. "I don't fare too well when I'm being teased."

"Oh. I see."

"Good." With that, Adrian quickly lifted her onto his desk,

planting her firm behind on the map. He nudged her legs apart with his hands, fitting himself comfortably between them, like he belonged there.

"Ooh!" Cory was loving Adrian's warm hands against the inside of her thighs. She ran her own hands down his muscular ones, reaching as far as she could but suddenly stopped short. She quickly moved her hands upward again after feeling the cold steel of his pistol still strapped to his right leg.

Instead, she focused her hands under his T-shirt, finally feeling firsthand his hard chest. Cory's eager hands roamed wantonly and hungrily over it. Smooth. Hard. Beautiful. Though she couldn't see them, the power she felt from his rock-hard abs seeped into her.

"Is everything okay down there?" Adrian stopped kissing her to ask.

"Oh, yeah. Perfect," she smiled.

"Okay," Adrian started unbuttoning her blouse, slowly. "Now it's my turn."

"Ummh," Cory moaned again as excitement gushed between her legs. She could tell by his movements that this man was definitely experienced. Adrian effortlessly removed her blouse and unclasped her bra and before long, she was completely topless. Cory shivered as the cold air of the room assaulted her bare breasts.

Adrian cupped them gently, warming them, stroking them, her small nipples instantly responding to his every touch and hardening even more so in his hands. Cory arched her back, inviting him to sample.

"These are really beautiful," he murmured. "And just the way I like them," he whispered against her neck. "Just thought you should know that."

"Oh, I like them too," Cory laughed softly.

Adrian tasted her nipple and when his wet tongue encircled it, Cory gave an even louder gasp. As he gently began to suck, her stomach clenched and she drew air into her lungs.

"Oh, Adrian," Cory finally managed, able to speak again. "This is so damn good."

"But I haven't even begun with you yet, Cory."

His tongue lingered, and more agonizing seconds ticked by before Adrian moved on to her other erect nipple, sucking even harder now as moan after moan consumed Cory.

"Now, how do *you* like being teased?" Adrian asked her when he surfaced for air.

"Mmm, I think I love it," Cory answered breathlessly.

"Do you have any idea how much I want you right now, Cory?" Adrian asked her.

"I do," she whispered.

As Adrian bent his head, a knock sounded on the door. He stopped in midair and just stood there looking at her, contemplating.

Then he sighed and grumbled, "One sec, Cory." He walked across the small room as the knock came again. Adrian unlocked and eased open the door. Thank God his tall frame and muscular shoulders almost filled the entire doorway so whoever it was wouldn't see her.

Cory hastily grabbed her blouse and pulled it over her shoulders. Her hands were trembling as she hurriedly began to button up. She quickly stuffed her chocolate-colored lace bra into her purse. She didn't have time to put that on right now. But her still erect nipples were pushing against the fabric of her blouse, still tingling from Adrian's hot lips.

"LT, there's a telephone call for you from Sergeant Jones," a male voice was saying.

"Thanks, private. I'm just finishing up lunch. Tell him I'll call him back."

"Okay, sir."

Whoever it was made a hasty retreat. When Adrian turned around again, Cory was standing with her blouse all intact. She was about to pick up her handbag when Adrian said, "Sorry 'bout that, Cory. Boy, you sure move swift!"

"You should talk," Cory laughed.

"And where do you think you're going?" Adrian asked, holding her possessively around her waist.

"You're a very busy man, it seems. Besides you have to finish your *lunch*, LT." Cory giggled.

"I was really, *really* enjoying my lunch," Adrian teased, causing her to blush all over.

"I should go. It's about time I get back to the office and I certainly have no intentions of getting arrested today."

"Arrested? For what?"

"Oh, I don't know. Inappropriate behavior on a military base perhaps? I'm sure you all will think of something," Cory teased. She was now trying to smooth her hair back but in vain.

"And who's going to arrest you? I certainly don't have any arresting powers."

"That may be so, but your friends in black sure do."

"Well, in that case, let me walk you out. Once you're with me, you'll be safe."

Cory believed him. She remembered how safe she had felt with him the other day. And after just now, she absolutely knew she was in good hands.

As they stepped outside Adrian's office, the coolness of the room quickly dissipated into the steamy atmosphere. Cory was finding it difficult to walk now. Between her legs was wet from their steamy lunch-time rendezvous. What just happened between them, she completely blamed on the weather. It was just too hot and steamy today and this man was just like the weather.

The handsome, charming, polite and not forgetting sexy-as-hell package that he was appealed to her even more now. But she distrusted men in uniform. Didn't she? She was probably getting delirious from all this heat.

More curious looks were directed at them as they walked toward Cory's car. Embarrassed now, she wondered if anyone besides Adrian had heard her moaning. She needed to get out of here, fast. When they finally reached her car, Adrian moved swiftly enough to open her door.

"So are we still on for tomorrow evening?" he asked, looking at her expectantly.

"Yep."

"Great. And Cory?"

"Yes?"

"I'm really glad you came by today."

"Me, too. So I'll see you tomorrow, then," Cory waved as she drove out the compound.

She felt like a slut. But a happy slut! Cory couldn't help what just happened here. She had come just to thank the guy and apologize. Not only did she manage to ask him out but she also found herself making out with him. In the middle of the day. On his desk. At a military base of all places! It seemed like she was losing her damn mind.

Chapter 9

The next day couldn't have come quickly enough for Cory. Technically, it wasn't really a date per se but she was going to see Adrian again. And after yesterday, who wouldn't? But this time in a different setting. One where they could finally sit across from each other and have a decent conversation over drinks. Especially one without guns and military uniforms, curious onlookers, and anything dark green. And one without a desk as well. Cory warmed all over as she remembered. But Adrian would be in her world now.

The sports bar she chose strategically because it was just next door to her office building and a cool walking distance. The American-style cuisine and casual dining atmosphere should make Adrian feel right at home, too. He had told her all about his shared heritage and ancestry. This she was already accustomed to; she, too, was the product of a biracial marriage. Though she was a native Trinidadian, Cory shared an African and East-Indian parentage, hence her extremely wild and curly hair.

She was almost half an hour early and was promptly seated at the bar. Okay, so maybe she was a little excited. She ordered her favorite cocktail, a sour apple martini, and waited on Adrian's arrival. As she sipped on the sweet and tangy drink, Cory reflected on all the men in her life now. There was her father, brother, and Jay. Then her gynecologist, who also happened to be her good friend as well as Elisha's husband, Curtis. A weird friendship some might say but an important one nonetheless. All of them served a specific purpose.

So any other man who may come waltzing into her life now would have one sole purpose—to physically satisfy her. Cory had everything all figured out. Why bother to go through all the troubles and hassles of a relationship when in the end, it all just boiled down to the damn sex, anyway?

She hadn't always thought this way. She had believed in the whole marriage thing before—the man of her dreams sweeping her off her feet, the magical proposal, the fancy house with the white picket fence, the two kids and two dogs dream. But all it took was one man, enough shed tears, and a broken heart to let go of all those.

So here she was, one asshole and three wasted years of her life later. But with a changed mindset. All she required now was a good orgasm after an extremely hard day ever so often. What she really needed was a man to knock her freaking boots off. And Cory believed the most promising candidate to more than likely fill this position should be joining her any minute now.

Above the rim of her martini glass, Cory saw Adrian approaching, his walk upright and purposeful like he couldn't wait to reach his destination, the sight of him totally not what she was expecting. If she thought he looked gorgeous in his military uniform, in civilian clothing, Adrian was even more striking. It was her very first time seeing him out of uniform, dressed casually in a black long-sleeved cotton shirt that was pulled snugly across his broad chest and slim dark blue jeans. Cory was experiencing flashes of its hardness where her hands freely roamed yesterday. Adrian looked—as she would usually say in Spanish—*muy caliente!*

"Hi, hope I didn't keep you waiting long?" Adrian bent his head to kiss her cheek, pulled out the bar stool opposite to Cory and sat. His lips were hot, burning her already flushed skin.

"No, you're on time," Cory answered, taking a long seductive sip of her martini.

"You look amazing as always, Cory."

"Thank you. You look really nice yourself. Like a normal civilian at last." In civilian clothing, Adrian was no soldier to her, and she it was easy to fool herself. And he smelled simply luscious. Cory had to ask something quickly to distract herself from becoming lost in the depths of those smoldering eyes and from that look he was giving her with them. She was normally on top of her game. She was usually the one who pushed the buttons in the opposite sex. Now, all it took was one look from this man and she got all flustered.

"So what would you like to have?" Cory asked.

Adrian smiled and started laughing. "About that," he began. "You know, Cory, I'm really not much of a drinker. Only on really special occasions do I have alcohol."

"Why didn't you just say something, then?" Cory wanted to just kick herself for not finding that out before asking him out. Then again, it was so spur of the moment. Besides, which man on this island didn't drink alcohol?

"Look, it's no big deal, really. And why would I want to jeopardize a chance of going out with such a beautiful woman?"

Cory blushed. "Don't be silly. You should have just said so."

Adrian finally settled on a local Carib beer. "For you, I'll drink paint if I have to today. And just so you know, I do consider this a very special occasion."

Cory felt a lot better sipping on her martini now. At least he didn't order fruit punch.

"To good times," Adrian raised his bottle to clink her glass.

Cory reciprocated the gesture. *To good times indeed*, she smiled. "*Salud!*"

Cory wanted to find out everything she could about him. They both sat and chatted for what seemed like hours as they dined on hot wings and celery sticks dipped in blue cheese dressing.

He was not only easy on the eyes; he was good on her body and mind. He was easy to talk to on just about anything.

Okay, so this didn't turn out to be one of those horror dates from hell where you just wanted to dash to the ladies' room and call up your girlfriends to come rescue you. Cory found herself having a really good time and from all signals Adrian was giving, he was too. But she really *needed* to go to the ladies' now.

*

When she excused herself, Adrian took notice of the short blue cotton shirt-dress she was wearing. She really did wear these vibrant Caribbean colors well. All he was able to see before were those luscious legs and calves. He had to admit, this woman sure did know how to get his blood pumping. Was she just trying to deliberately drive him insane?

Adrian's eyes never left Cory's swaying behind as she walked off because she sure as hell knew how to sway those hips with conviction. As Adrian watched her go, a waitress came over to his side of the bar, interrupting his thoughts.

"Can I get you anything else?" she asked cheerfully, sweetly.

"No, thank you, ma'am," he responded, never taking his eyes off Cory's backside.

"Are you sure?" she asked again. "Anything at all?"

Okay, was she offering more than what was on the menu here? Adrian thought he was right about that hint in her voice and that smile she was wearing.

"No, I'm fine, ma'am," he insisted as he turned to face her this time. "Actually, you could bring me the bill."

The visibly disappointed looking waitress left without saying another word. Adrian sat and waited till Cory emerged from the ladies'.

"I'm back," she announced.

"I missed you already," Adrian quipped. Then he realized just how much of a good time he was having with her. Cory was a ray of bright sunshine lighting up his evening. When the waitress finally brought the bill, she all but slammed it down on the bar counter. She then flashed Cory The Look and left.

Cory smiled mischievously; she must have realized what was going on. "Was that waitress just hitting on you?" she inquired.

Adrian just grinned at her, shrugging his shoulders. He

instinctively dipped into his pocket to reach for his wallet but Cory promptly stopped him, unconsciously resting her hand on his arm.

"Oh, no you don't. What're you doing? I invited you out, remember?"

Not wanting to insult her further, Adrian backed down and allowed Cory to foot the bill.

"Okay, you win. This is just so strange for me, though."

"Adrian, we *are* in the twenty-first century!" Cory insisted after swiping her credit card and making the payment.

"I guess we are."

*

Not wanting to leave him yet, Cory asked Adrian to walk her to her car that was still parked at her office. Not that she expected anything less of him. She had to admit, she was pleasantly surprised at how mannerly, polite, and gentlemanly he always was.

It was one of those hot, balmy nights on the island. They walked side by side. The usual night breezes were slow in coming. The car park was just a short distance away, so Cory ensured she took her sweet time in getting there. She turned it into a very slow and sexy stroll with Adrian.

A gentle breeze blew past, rippling through her curly hair. Cory stopped arms outstretched, enjoying the feel of it cooling her face and legs.

"So how come you still live with your parents?" he asked her after a while.

"Huh . . . that's a long story," she sighed. "My mom was diagnosed with breast cancer so I moved back home to be with her and spend more time with her and to help out my dad. When she died, I just didn't leave again." It was so much easier for Cory to talk about her mother's death. It was natural. But Collin's death? His was too unnatural to discuss with anyone and it was still much too painful to even try.

"I had to take care of my dad and my younger brother still has to finish high school," Cory explained. "So that was that and here I am two years later and still living at home. Pathetic, I know."

"I'm really sorry to hear about your mom. That must've been really hard on you."

"You have no idea. And to top it off, my dad treats me like I'm still five years old."

"Hey, you can't really blame the man. After all, he has such a beautiful daughter. He's just looking out for you like any father should. Besides, Caribbean parents have a harder time letting go of their kids, it seems. The longer they could keep you living under their roof, the better."

"Yeah, that's so true," Cory said.

"Imagine, my cousin's forty and he still lives with his parents."

"So I have hope yet," Cory burst out laughing. "I mean, I love my father and brother to death but sometimes they just love to make me scream."

"If I had a daughter, she wouldn't be able to speak to boys till she's like fifty," Adrian said. "But honestly, though, I think it's really commendable. That you were there for your family when they needed you most."

"Thank you," Cory said. "It means a lot to hear somebody say that."

"It's important, for me at least, to know the people you love most have your back when need be," he said.

Adrian sounded very serious now, a little pained, too. Cory noticed his tone changing. She wondered what that was all about but didn't ask.

When they finally reached her car, and Adrian opened her door, there was that exciting feeling approaching. He was standing so close, his face just mere inches away. He touched her on her cheek and stroked it gently. Cory shivered. How she yearned and craved Adrian's body touching hers again. It was incredible how he could ignite her entire body with just a single touch. She could smell the cologne on his shirt as he came closer. Cory tiptoed, meeting him on the half.

Adrian lowered his head for a kiss. His hand settled on her bare leg as it slid under her dress, playing with the smooth, cool flesh underneath.

"I'll follow you home," he muttered against Cory's lips.

"*What?*" Cory was in shock. Her eyes immediately flew open. She hadn't been expecting to hear that. "You don't have to," an out-of-breath Cory replied. Her legs felt like they had no bones left in them, threatening to give way at any moment. Thank God she had her good old car to lean against.

"No, but I want too. I need to know you're safe."

"No, really, it's not necessary."

"Cory, could you please allow me to do this?"

"Okay, I'd love the security detail, Adrian," she laughed.

In the rearview mirror, Cory noticed Adrian right behind her all the way during the careful drive to her house. She'd had a few casual dates before this one and not one of the guys ever offered to follow her home. Cory was shocked that he was actually following her all the way to Lange Park and more shocked that he hadn't invited her over to his place.

She wondered what it was that was holding him back from doing so. Was he not interested in being with her? Why was he driving all the way to her house knowing full well that she still lived with her father and brother? They could have easily gone to his place right in the city.

Her lips were still burning from that kiss and those apple martinis had her so damn horny right now. Every time he looked at her she felt the chemistry between them. Or was it purely lust on her part? She was going insane from want. She had to find out sooner or later what Adrian's whole hang-up was because after tonight, she most definitely had plans for him.

Adrian strolled up to her as she was getting out of the car.

"Well, thank you for the security detail. And everything else," Cory beamed at him.

"It was my pleasure, ma'am. I'm here ready and willing to serve you," he said, a gleam in his eyes.

And she was ready and willing to be served. God, did he always have to sound so damn sexy, too?

"Sweet dreams, Cory."

Cory waved as she opened the door to her house. It was probably the first time the poor guy had followed a twenty-six-year-old, grown-ass woman all the way home to her father's house after a date, she thought miserably. If it were anybody else, he would have been busy getting his freak on right about now.

This depressing thought only gave her renewed vigor to find her own place even sooner, starting tomorrow. She would have probably been in heaven at about now, she fumed. Thank God her father wasn't up and about. Knowing him, he would have only added to her misery and interrogated her about her whereabouts. He constantly reminded her of what happened to Collin. Well, that was the small price you had to pay for living under your father's roof still.

*

As Adrian was driving back to the city, he was thinking of how the times had changed. How women were now asking the men out, paying for the dates, initiating all the moves, proposing, the whole nine yards. They were no longer dependent on men for anything it seemed. It was as if they no longer needed a man in their life. Except for one thing, probably. And still men had competition in that arena.

Gone were the good old days of picking up your date at her home, meeting her parents, being interrogated by her father, making out in your car, bringing her home, and then making out some more. The tables were indeed turning. Relationships were just like a game waiting to be played these days. But now, the players were the ones being played by the women.

And somehow he didn't seem to mind when it was Cory. That was when he knew he was getting himself dangerously too close to her. Well, she wasn't just any woman, that was for sure. Cory was the entire package you brought home to your mother. She had the looks, the body, the confidence, the independence, the ambition, the personality. All the things he found to be incredibly sexy and attractive in a woman.

Was all this just the loneliness or boredom creeping up on him? Though his routine boredom was quickly disappearing since meeting her. He had instantly felt a strong sexual tension between them. That body of hers was just begging to be touched. And the way Cory had responded to him yesterday . . . Adrian knew he had a job to finish. He still wanted her so badly.

However, he had no intention of getting emotionally entangled with her. It wasn't just his work that made it difficult to think of settling down, it was also that Cory had no problems making it known how she felt about guys like him. That didn't mean he would stop seeing her. He knew exactly what she needed from him and he had every intention of giving her exactly that. No, it was his duty to give her exactly what she needed and that was all it was going to be.

Chapter 10

Cory awoke the next morning to the sounds of a painful and irritating banging in her head. She only had three sour apple martinis last night and now she was paying for it. She wandered to the kitchen to get water for an aspirin and still didn't see anyone around. Looked like she would have the house all to herself for a while. Oh, how she missed living alone.

Her father had probably gone to the supermarket. Her brother, Christian, on the other hand, she hadn't a clue. She didn't know if he still lived in this house or not, actually. Cory had no idea where he was at any given day. What else could you really expect from an eighteen-year-old? She remembered the things she'd done when she was Christian's age. She had started university and was finally away from her parents' clutches.

She took the pill and made a steaming cup of coffee. Back in her bedroom, she thought of Adrian, since the aspirin was taking rather long to kick in. If anything else could ease her pain, she knew it would be thoughts of him. She grabbed her cell phone to call him. The call went straight to voicemail and she was in no mood to leave a message.

Her brain madly drifted in all different directions, making her head pound even more. She was right. She knew his type. The tall, gorgeous, charming, player type. The smiling, sweet-talking until he got what he wanted type. The only wanted to pull down your panties type. This reminded her of an e-mail she'd received from Gabby the other day, "Wherever there's a good-looking, sweet, single man, there's some woman who's tired of his bullshit."

For her sake, Cory wanted something to be definitely wrong with Adrian before she made a fool of herself . . . again. Please God, let him be married or have a child or two baby mamas somewhere, a STD, six toes, hell something . . . anything. Anything to stop these crazy thoughts from surfacing in her head.

Only Adrian never once showed any signs of any of those things last night. No, it didn't matter anyway. Adrian Mendez definitely wasn't her type. Well, at least that was what she kept telling herself over the entire weekend. *So why then are you always responding like that to his every touch?*

The rest of the weekend flew by quickly as she checked the classifieds for an apartment rental. It was about time she got her freak on again. Cory saw only a few places that interested her. They met her requirements of being in the suburbs around the capital city, close to her job to cut back on her work commute, two bedrooms, furnished, and pretty much close to everything. Of course the rental price was an entirely different issue altogether as prices in and around the city were astronomical compared to other areas on the island.

Before she knew it, it was Monday morning again and back to the grind. Getting up before the crack of dawn and having to brace the early morning rush hour traffic to get to her office and then again having to face it back home on evenings was torture.

Then there was work and more work to get done at the office. Javier needed to get everything now. Not to mention the added pressure he put on her probably just because he could. He ran the department as if the islanders were still ruled by the colonial government under Her Majesty of Spain. At least, that was what she told him once. Javier made it his job to irritate the hell out of her every day after that.

Cory was busy putting the finishing touches on a speech she'd prepared for him to give at a cocktail reception being held by the Spanish ambassador on the island. She had been behind all morning because he just had to make a million and one changes to it. Probably just to spite or irritate her. The man was killing the Amazon forest, the amount of paper she'd used for this speech already.

It was about one in the afternoon and Cory hadn't even eaten any lunch yet when she received a call from the receptionist downstairs.

"Just tell him he'll get it in five minutes, okay," Cory snapped.

"What? Tell who they'll get what?" Rachel, the receptionist, asked.

"Oh, sorry, Rachel. Sorry for snapping at you. Javier is up my ass again."

"I see," Rachel laughed. "Anyway, you have to come downstairs immediately."

"Why? I can't right now. I have to finish his stupid speech." Even though she was now an assistant manager, Cory was still functioning in the capacity of Javier's executive assistant. Since the world recession hit and the oil price fell drastically, the company was cutting back on almost everything in order to trim costs to survive this economic downturn.

Besides working under this very disgusting Spanish expat manager, handling two separate job portfolios, working ten-hour days and being severely overworked in the process, it was amazing how Cory still managed to love her job. At least she was afforded every other Friday off as a perk. And at least she and Jay had jobs to complain about during lunch.

"Look, just come down right this minute," Rachel demanded. She still didn't give Cory a reason but she sounded excited. "It'll be worth your while, I promise."

"Okay, fine."

Cory hung up the phone and took the elevator down. She hoped whatever it was wouldn't be a waste of her precious, limited time. Cory entered the reception lobby and the first thing she saw was a huge floral bouquet.

"These are for you," Rachel beamed, presenting the flowers to her like she'd just won the first prize in a beauty pageant. There were beautiful orange lilies, yellow and white orchids, and tall birds of paradise flowers with other greens filled in between. Cory loved flowers and this beautiful vase touched her.

"You're so lucky, Cory. And to think it's not even Valentine's

Day yet," Rachel went all romantic-sounding on her. "So . . . who are they from? You must share."

Cory inhaled the divine scent of the lilies. Receiving flowers at the office was nothing new to her but when she opened the card she gasped. It simply read, *Cory, thanks for making me laugh. I had a great time the other night. Adrian.* So it was Adrian who sent her these gorgeous flowers?

All the while Rachel was busy cooing away. "Ooh, how sweet. Cory, this guy must really like you."

"Nah, it's nothing like that," she responded. She didn't bother to tell Rachel the details and that it was she who had asked Adrian out in the first place.

As soon as she put the huge arrangement down on her desk and reached for her cell phone, Jay came waltzing in and comfortably plunked himself down on her visitor's chair.

"So who's the lucky, pussy-whipped fella?" he asked, grinning from ear to ear.

"He isn't pussy-whipped. Yet."

"But let me make a wild guess. It's from your ass-admiring soldier, isn't it?"

"Yes, Jay. Now could you get back to your office and do some work. I'm very busy."

Ignoring Cory, Jay began rubbing his hands together. "Just think, Cory, if soldier boy plays his cards right, I'll finally be free."

"You're such an idiot. Get out, please," Cory demanded.

As soon as Jay left, she dialed Adrian's number. Javier would just have to wait a few minutes more. She was feeling a bit apprehensive but still waited, listening as the phone rang. A handsome low voice with an American accent answered this time. Cory sighed in relief. It was the same familiar voice she heard in her head every night since she first met him. It was the same sensations she felt every time it rained and every time her heart beat quickened. This voice warmed her all over.

"Hello, gorgeous," Adrian answered.

"Hi, I just called to say thank you for the beautiful flowers."

"Oh, but what makes you think that I had anything to do with that?" he joked.

"Maybe because you signed your name at the end of the card."

"Damn girl, somebody must have forged my signature."

"So what're you doing right now?" Cory asked.

"Working like you."

"Chasing car thieves?" she joked. It was Adrian's turn to laugh now. They spoke some more and after wishing her a beautiful afternoon, he ended the call. Cory had the broadest smile on her face when she hung up the phone. The rest of her day went incredibly great. Neither Javier's rants of her tardiness could spoil it for her nor his other million changes to the speech that afternoon.

Chapter 11

On Saturday, the entire atmosphere in Trinidad was buzzing with pre-Carnival excitement. Cory loved this time of year, with activities and different parties every night.

She and her friends Elisha, Gabrielle, and Kerry were attending one of the biggest Carnival parties of the season, featuring Trinidad's finest and most spectacular soca artiste. Machel Montano's music was both infectious and energetic and Cory loved it. The party was a fashionable affair filled with animated conversations, loud laughter, and fun. There was nothing better than going out with her girls and having a good time.

When they entered the stadium, the place was already packed to capacity with thousands of people. The atmosphere was electrifying and there was a certain excitement in the air tonight that completely energized Cory. The four bought some drinks and sipped on them and their bodies slowly gave in to the sensuous soca rhythms. They swayed in sweet abandon to the pulsating music that represented Carnival in sweet Trinidad and Tobago.

*

Adrian was not a happy camper to be working at this party tonight. He wanted to be partying himself. Unfortunately, he had lost a bet and this was his punishment. He hated crowd control. Their job was to ensure all party-goers were safe and physically restrain the ones that wanted to start any trouble.

At least there was lots of eye candy for the guys to feast upon. There were many beautiful, not to mention very sexy, women everywhere they looked. And as they were making the usual rounds of the venue, one of them caught Adrian's eye. A woman with crazy hair dressed in a very short pair of denims and tall black boots.

Cory? Adrian could never miss those wild curls anywhere. Neither the sultry movements of those hips. But he had to be sure.

She was definitely having a great time with her friends around her. They were all laughing and chatting and swaying their bodies, all a bit too provocatively.

"Guys, this way," Adrian shouted as he headed in the direction of the curly hair. As the line of them was passing, people in the crowd were moving briskly aside to clear a path for them. The smart ones obviously didn't want to mess with the heavily armed militia tonight.

"Give me a minute," Adrian announced when he stopped. All the others in line immediately stopped and waited on him. Adrian went up to her and whispered her name.

An excited Cory jumped and spun around. "Adrian," she exclaimed. Her arms instinctively flew around his neck.

Her reaction took Adrian quite by surprise. Not that he minded one bit. Clearly, she'd had a few drinks already.

"Hey, I didn't expect to see you here," Adrian finally managed to say. He was busy drinking in her sweetness. Her shorts were hugging her shapely hips and that top she was wearing clearly didn't require a bra. All the women around him ensured they dressed their sexiest at these parties and he wasn't one to complain. His eyes were transfixed on Cory, however, the only object of his desire.

"I don't miss this for the world," Cory was beaming.

Adrian finally looked at the other women in Cory's group.

"Oh, how rude of me. Adrian, these are my girls. This is Elisha, Gabrielle, and Kerry," Cory announced, pointing out each one of them after she called their names. Girls, this is Second Lieutenant Adrian Mendez."

"Ladies, it's a pleasure," Adrian briskly dipped his head as they all sang hi in unison. Then he bent and whispered again to Cory, "So I'll see you soon, Cory?"

"I'll try my very best," she whispered back.

Adrian smiled at them and continued on his way through the thick crowds, quickly followed by the others.

*

"Okay, could somebody please explain to me what all that lusting was all about just now," Gabby dramatically enquired as soon as Adrian left. Cory apparently wasn't the only drama queen in business.

"Yeah, Cory, who the hell is that?" Kerry piped in.

Cory licked her lips and tried to wipe the stupid look off her face. "That's Adrian, I told you all," she said.

"Adrian? Who's Adrian?" Kerry asked again.

"That, my dear friends, is the man who sent her flowers the other day," Elisha interjected.

"Hold up. He sent you flowers? And we're only now hearing about this?" Kerry asked.

"Wait! Just in case you all missed this and didn't realize, that man who was practically eating out of your ear is a soldier. *A heavily armed* soldier, too," Gabby exclaimed.

"Yeah, well, he's always armed," Cory calmly offered.

"That's right! Cory, since when are you into soldiers and men of arms?" Kerry asked, looking puzzled. "The last time I checked, you hated men in uniform."

"I am *not* into soldiers, okay," Cory vehemently remarked. She lied. She was definitely into this one. She loved the intensity with which Adrian did things. At least the intensity with which he always looked at her with those beautiful brown eyes of his. He looked at her as if no one else was around. As if only the two of them existed on this earth. Making his intentions well known to her without even uttering a word.

"So what was that all about, then?" an inquisitive Kerry was asking and jolting Cory from her thoughts.

"We all have to admit it. That man is hot, girlfriends," Gabby blurted.

"He sure is, girl," Cory excitedly added. "And the things he can do with those lips. . . ." Realizing what she was about to say, she stopped herself and trailed off.

"What did you just say? I must be tripping because I just thought I heard you say that you kissed the guy," Kerry said.

"Oh, it was a little more than that actually," Cory announced casually.

All three of their jaws dropped in surprise.

"Okay, it looks like you have some explaining to do, young lady," Elisha was able to rush out first.

"Fine, but after the party," Cory said.

"No. Now, please. We want you to share all the juicy details," Gabby said, rubbing her hands together.

"Fine," Cory said. So she finally told her friends all about Adrian and how they'd met. And of course, everyone had their opinions on the matter, as would be expected with girlfriends.

"But you know how men are. They're only interested in sleeping with you. And that look soldier boy just gave you, spelled it out loud and clear," Gabby, the oldest of the four and the harshest where men were concerned, was the first to give her two cents.

"And what if that's what I'm interested in as well?" Cory interjected.

"And since when are you into the whole casual sex thing, Cory?" Elisha asked. She had a certain degree of alarm in her tone. Probably because she was the only one in the group happily married.

"Since this year," Cory responded. "Remember this was all your idea in the first place, for me to find a man for the New Year?"

"Yeah, but not the first one that comes along. Or not one that makes you just want to climb into bed with him, Cory," Elisha explained in her signature lecturer's voice.

"Oh my God, Cory. I can't believe you're falling for that BS. This is the epitome of a player. The charm, the flowers, the random acts of kindness. Girl, are you really falling for all that?" Gabby enquired. "He probably only found your damn car so that you'd sleep with him."

"Oh, Gabby, you sound just like Jay," Cory retorted.

"And what exactly did Jay have to say about all this?" Gabby asked. "Just out of curiosity."

"Looks like soldier boy's working overtime to hit that ass," Cory said in her best Jay impersonation.

"Yep. That sounds like a typical Jay comment," Gabby laughed.

"And steps one, two, and three, direct from the *Players Handbook*," Elisha added, backing up Gabby's point. At this, everyone erupted into loud laughter, all except for Kerry. She was the only one just listening in on the conversation now.

"Although I have to admit, the casual sex thing is good. As long as you can keep your heart out of it," Gabby interjected.

"And that's coming from the queen of casual sex," Elisha hastily added.

"You and a soldier, Cory?" Kerry finally broke her silence. "I just can't see the both of you together. What could you two possibly have in common?"

"Look, maybe we need to change our perceptions about military men," Cory reasoned.

"*We*? I don't believe this crap," Kerry exploded, sounding annoyed as hell.

"What's your problem, Kerry?" Cory demanded, beginning to sound a little annoyed herself.

"My problem? Oh, you're so freaking unbelievable, Cory. It was *you* all along who had that problem ever since Collin's death," she shouted. "And now for some strange reason, one comes along with an American accent and you can't wait to do him!"

For the first time everyone in the group went completely silent. They all understood Collin's death was a never-talked-about topic for Cory. After what seemed like forever, she finally broke the silence. "Well, maybe I'm starting to see things differently now, Kerry."

"And I suppose we should all be grateful for that, right?" And with that Kerry stormed off, pushing her way through the thick crowd, much to everyone's total disbelief.

Chapter 12

Another hectic and stressful work week greeted Cory. She stopped and took a minute to gaze through the windows from her office overlooking the Queens Park Savannah just across the street. How she loved this magnificent overhead view that offered so much for her to lose her thoughts in.

Cory's thoughts were interrupted by the buzz of her cell phone vibrating on the desk. When she looked at the screen, Adrian's name was flashing across it. She immediately grabbed it. This was just the right kind of distraction she needed.

"Hi, gorgeous. What's up?" Adrian asked.

"I'm fine now that I'm hearing your voice," Cory teased. Now it was her turn to flirt with him. "Because right now, I'm so stressed out, I can't even think clearly."

"Well, how 'bout I take care of that stress for you?"

What was he asking here? "Hmmm, your offer sounds rather tempting."

"So what're you doing this evening?"

"Oh, I have plans," Cory blurted out without even thinking. Anyway, that was good so that he wouldn't think she was just sitting around waiting for him to call.

"Okay. Maybe we could hook up some other time, then?"

"On second thought. It's nothing really special. I was just going jogging, that's all," Cory hurriedly interjected.

"That sounds like a great way to relieve that stress. Will you mind if a soldier joins you on his day off?"

"Only if he could keep up with me," Cory teased.

Adrian was already waiting across the street from her office building when she came outside a little after five. He was definitely a man on time. Cory figured it had to do with his military training. She was impressed nevertheless.

"Hey," he waved to her as she crossed the street. Adrian was sitting on the beautiful black wrought-iron railings that wound its way around the entire Savannah.

"Hi." Cory came across quite breathless. Not because she'd just run across the street but because Adrian had just kissed her on her cheek. "Shall we?" she asked. "I've been waiting all afternoon for this." Cory was telling the truth.

The Savannah was packed with avid walkers and joggers, the main reason being the fast-approaching Carnival. Everyone wanted to look their best for the two-day festival and to keep up with the strenuous pace of the street parade. Both Cory and Adrian were flanked by bodies of all shapes and sizes ranging from the very sexy and physically fit ones to those in need of losing the extra Christmas pounds.

The towering poui trees lined their path with a carpet of soft and pretty pink and yellow petals. They started walking at first, making small talk with each other along the way as Gothic churches, historic buildings, the U.S. Embassy, the Zoo, and the President's House all came into their view. They spoke about their day and week so far, about the extremely hot weather and Carnival coming up.

For a Marine, Adrian was so soft-spoken and such a gentleman. Weren't soldiers supposed to be loud and rough and arrogant? Then wasn't *he* supposed to be loud and rough and arrogant, too? Although he did have the physical signs—the height and muscular-toned body and the four letters, USMC, tattooed on his left arm, Cory knew Adrian was anything but rough.

Only, he couldn't be the same man who had kissed her so softly or caressed her cheek or stroked her breasts ever so gently with that same big hand, filling her body and mind with mad desire for him . . . Cory didn't understand how he managed to pull this off. How could this man still be so gentle?

Adrian must have been asking her something while she was busy daydreaming away because he was looking very curiously at her now.

"What?" Cory asked.

"I was just wondering what had you smiling like that," he said.

"I wasn't smiling," she offered with a smile.

"See. It was just like that," Adrian laughed.

Cory took off running, leaving Adrian trailing behind. She felt like she needed to run . . . fast.

"Hey, maybe you shouldn't do that just yet," Adrian called after her. When he pulled up at her side once more, he asked, "So you really think you could keep up with me, Cory?"

Cory knew Adrian was trained for this kind of stuff but she couldn't help herself, she just had to tease him some more.

"Oh, I think you may not be able to keep up with me, soldier boy!" Then she picked up her pace another notch and left him again.

She hadn't gotten far when she felt a burning pain in her leg and pulled up sharply, crying out. Adrian reached her in an instant. Cory was trying to keep the weight off her injured leg and was cursing loudly. Already other curious joggers were slowing down, taking in the show.

Adrian held her arm and enquired, "Cory, are you alright?"

"No. I think I just pulled something," she replied, grimacing in pain.

"Where does it hurt?" he asked, his voice etched with sudden concern for her.

"My leg."

"Hmm. Did you do any stretches before, Cory?"

"Yeah." She lied.

"Come sit over here for a while." Adrian helped her as she hopped to one of the empty benches that lined the joggers' path. He gently lifted her right leg out. "Show me where it hurts now."

Cory jumped, not from the grimacing pain this time but from the heat of Adrian's touch on her calf.

"Where does it hurt, Cory?" Adrian asked again.

"My leg. Up here," she responded pointing.

"I'm almost positive you pulled a muscle in your thigh," he said knowingly. "Is the pain throbbing more from behind?"

"Yes."

"You think you could walk on it?"

"I don't know."

"Look, I need to go get my pickup, then. You have to rest that leg a bit. I'll just run and get it now."

"No! Don't leave me here," Cory said. They had already walked almost three quarter way around the circumference of the three-and-a-half kilometers Queen's Park Savannah.

"I'll be really quick. I promise. I'm parked not too far from here," Adrian insisted. "Either that or I'll have to carry you myself." He smiled when he saw the look of horror flash across her face and said, "I thought so."

"Okay, hurry back then," Cory said.

"Yes, ma'am." Adrian saluted and continued running in a quick sprint in the same direction.

Cory was left feeling like a complete fool sitting on the bench, mentally cursing herself for being stupid enough not to warm up first. But she got so excited when she saw Adrian that she forgot all about that. Now she was paying a very painful price indeed. She just felt like disappearing now. Maybe she should just hop back to her office. Nah. That would probably attract even more attention. The suitable thing to do was sit and wait for Adrian to come back.

After a few minutes, he pulled up with his vehicle.

"Missed me?" Adrian asked.

"You were so quick, I don't think I had enough time to," Cory answered.

Adrian opened the door behind his driver's seat. Before she could protest, he swooped her into his arms and was about to lift her into his pickup.

"I need to sweep you off your feet a bit," he joked.

Her face was incredibly close to his now. Cory wondered if Adrian could hear her loud heartbeats. "What? Where're we going?" she protested.

"I'm taking you to my place, so you can put your legs up for a while."

When Cory giggled at his statement, he retracted. "No, wait. Please allow me to rephrase that. I think you should keep *off your feet* for a while. You certainly can't drive right now," he quickly added. "And I don't live too far from here."

Cory knew Adrian was probably right. She didn't argue or needed any further coaxing on the matter.

"Don't worry, I won't do anything you don't want me to," Adrian smiled sweetly and looked all angelic at her.

Something suddenly caught in her throat. "You promise?" Cory asked.

"I promise. Boy Scouts honor."

He put Cory down on the back seat and closed the door. Then he got behind the wheel.

He didn't lie when he said he lived close by. They drove for all of two minutes when Adrian pulled off the Savannah's circumference and headed down onto St. Clair Avenue.

The suburbs of St. Clair was one of the more illustrious neighborhoods on the island, known for its prized mansions, new high-rise apartments, sprawling townhouses, and expensive condos. Cory wasn't even in his apartment yet and she was already impressed.

Adrian made a left and pulled in front of a massive gateway that was already opening via a remote he had pressed. It looked like a newly built architectural dream. Opposite was the King George the Fifth Park. Just like the Savannah, it was busy with all forms of exercise enthusiasts. Adrian quickly parked and helped her out.

Cory didn't notice anyone around, except for a lone guard who secured the white Mediterranean-styled building with its open verandahs overlooking the park. She quickly counted six stories on the beautiful building. Maybe soon, she'd be living in an apartment like this one, Cory thought as Adrian effortlessly lifted her into his arms again and carried her toward the elevator on the ground floor. This apartment building was right smack in the middle of everything: the malls, restaurants, gyms, the hottest night spots, and even a private hospital.

Her heart leapt in her chest when Adrian opened the door and switched on the lights.

"So this is where you live?" Cory asked the obvious. The room looked so cozy when she glanced about. She couldn't explain the nervous shiver she momentarily felt, though. Was it because Adrian had finally brought her to his place or was it because the inside of the apartment was so cool? Not that this was remotely close to the real reason she wanted to be here.

"Yep." Adrian set her down carefully on a plush brown sofa. "I'll be right back," he said and took off down a hallway.

He came back bearing a small medicine kit in his hands.

"I knew you'd have one of these things," Cory joked.

"This is a sports balm, okay?" Adrian took out the small red bottle and opened it. "Let me warn you, it'll burn a bit at first and then turn really cold. But trust me, it works."

"Well, as long as it works fast. I still have to drive home."

Adrian sat at the other end of the sofa and gently removed her running shoes and socks for her. "Only if you really want to," he added softly.

Was that an invitation?

"I think you'll need to roll that up," he said, pointing at her navy blue three-quarter running tights.

"Oh, I'm sorry," a distracted Cory offered as she pulled up the tights. He deftly but gently began to massage the balm into her sore leg muscle. All the while, she remained very rigid on the sofa, afraid to move or even speak. The heat from the rub began to scorch her skin—or was that from Adrian's hands moving up and down her leg? Exciting her with every deliberate stroke he made. Cory wondered what his strong hands would feel like massaging other parts of her body.

Adrian really needed to stop this now. "Does anywhere else hurt?" he was asking, jolting Cory from her dreaming again.

"Yes . . . I mean no!"

Adrian looked up at her. "Are you sure?"

"Yes!"

"Not to worry then, I think you'll live. Just relax here for a while and rest that leg. It should be good in a few more minutes."

She was now comfortably propped up on his sofa with her legs outstretched. "That massage did the trick, I think. It feels really good already. You're very good with your hands . . . at massaging, that is," Cory was quick to add.

Adrian smiled and shook his head.

"You know, I have to admit something to you," Cory whispered. Adrian's apartment was so quiet, she felt compelled to whisper.

"And what's that?" Adrian whispered back.

"I didn't warm up before."

"I knew it," he loudly exclaimed as he exasperatedly flung his hands into the air.

"Come on." And Cory thought she was dramatic? "I was running with a Marine for the first time in my life so I wanted to show you how fit I was. I really didn't mean to cause you so much trouble, Adrian."

"You could have seriously injured yourself." Adrian shook his head and added, "Cory, I could see how amazingly fit you are already. No need to kill yourself in the process to prove it to me."

"Thanks," she said.

"You're most welcome," Adrian returned. "So since we're on the topic of admitting things . . . I gotta admit, you have the most amazing legs . . . so firm and smooth," he said in a voice that was so sexy to her, his eyes never leaving hers. "Do you uh, weight train? Because your legs are so well defined."

Cory felt all flushed out. She was sure she changed color, from brown to bright red. "Sweet talking me won't get you anywhere, you know," she laughed. This guy was definitely trying to charm her pants off. Not that she minded.

"I know. I realized that since we met," Adrian was saying. "But actually, I *am* serious. You're a very beautiful woman, Cory. An exotic sun-kissed island goddess to be exact."

What the hell was she doing? Cory kept reminding herself that Adrian wasn't her type, yet here she was propped up on the man's sofa listening to him call her a goddess. An urgent and maddening rush of anticipation made her head spin and caused her to stop thinking as clearly as she was accustomed to. Maybe it was the smell of the sports balm. *Oh sure, Cory, since when did sports balm ever make anybody horny?*

"I'm going to take a quick shower," Adrian announced. She nodded, hardly able to speak.

Chapter 13

When she heard the shower come on, she used the opportunity to scour the room for anything that could tell her more about Adrian's life. He hardly ever spoke of himself unless she asked him something specifically. She noticed a photo of a smiling older woman on a wall. Then another with a woman and two young boys. There was also an old one with a soldier lifting a little boy. Probably Adrian when he was a child, Cory figured. He was a very cute little boy, too.

She figured they were his parents, sister, and nephews he always spoke so highly of. The younger woman's face looked so familiar. Cory got off the sofa and hobbled over to the photo hanging on the wall to get a better look. Up close, Cory felt like she knew the person but for the life of her, she couldn't figure it out.

Since she was already up, she decided to get some water from the nearby kitchen sink. Her leg was feeling a whole lot better already. As Cory passed an opened doorway, she stopped thinking of drinking water and started thinking of the water splashing from the shower and onto Adrian's lean body. Then, her feet began following the sounds of the shower instead. She entered the open doorway to his bedroom and stood there.

Adrian's gorgeous naked body. Water running all the way down. That was all she could think about. Cory didn't know what was going on with her head these days. First she blamed it on the weather. Then it was her raging, underused libido and now, sports balm? If only she would just admit that Adrian was so hot and she wanted him so badly. That she was scorching hot for this soldier. Angry with herself for being so lustful yes, but nevertheless, scorching hot for him still!

Cory licked her parched lips. She could really do with that drink now. The urge was just too much. She was done fighting with herself. She couldn't resist Adrian anymore. Her damn panties were completely drenched. Cory began moving closer and closer to the sound of the running water coming from his shower.

In a trance-like mode, she stepped into Adrian's bedroom. The first thing that got her attention was his massive four-poster bed made from some rich dark wood. As she touched one of the posts, Cory couldn't help but wonder about the many women she was sure Adrian pleasured in it. At least his bed was well made. That was a good sign.

The big bed was the center of attraction as far as the room's décor went because Adrian's bedroom was quite large but sparsely decorated. Its dark green walls made the space seem like some sort of dark, enchanted forest. There were two bedside tables with lamps on them, a huge flat-screen positioned on one of the walls and a walk-in closet. Both lamps were on, providing the only light in the room, casting a dim, sensuous glow across the bed that looked like a huge block of sinful dark chocolate. Talk about temptation!

Cory opened the door to Adrian's en-suite and entered. She saw him standing there through the clear glass doors. One hand rested on the wall, the other at his side. He seemed to be really enjoying the water. She froze, pondering her next move.

Then Cory slowly pulled the door and stepped inside the shower with him, the closeness of Adrian's naked body incensing her arousal even more. The intoxicating masculine scent of his shower gel stung her nostrils. The delicious cleanness of his glistening body was too much for her to resist. That was when she saw his other tattoos. A long snake menacingly wound its way down the center of Adrian's back, its tail ending just at his waist. *Well, of course he'd have tattoos, Cory. He was in the Marines, after all.*

When Cory touched his back, Adrian slowly turned. Cory jumped in surprise. There were even more tattoos. He had the head of a cobra snake tattooed on the left side of his chest. Why would he have a snake so close to his heart? Cory wondered. After closer inspection, she realized it was the continuation of the snake from down his back. The animal looked deadly with its wide-opened jaw, fangs leaping out at her. Cory swallowed. She hated snakes.

The tattoos and snakes were not all that had her gawking. She found pleasure, liking what she saw as her gaze wandered lower. Cory was finally able to see Adrian's rock hard abs and big strong chest, among other enticing things. He looked delectably chiseled and carved and so well formed. She was admiring his huge erection, drinking it all in with her roving eyes. She moved closer to him and curled her hands safely around his neck. His body felt so hard against hers.

The shower was still on. The warmness of the sprinkling water surprised Cory but it only added to igniting the fire between her legs. She was half expecting it to be cold. Now she was totally drenched but didn't care, her hair and clothing clung to her body. Cory tiptoed and whispered, "Do you mind if I join you, lieutenant?"

Adrian's eyes never left hers. He inhaled sharply as she held his erect manhood in her hand, teasing him.

He whispered back, "Only if you could handle what may happen to you if you do."

"I could handle anything."

"Oh, I believe you, Cory." And without another cue, Adrian turned the shower off.

"That's quite an amazing tattoo you got there," Cory said. She had to admit, it was an impressive work of art. She traced the pattern of the snake down his back with her fingertip. "A bit scary but impressive."

"Don't worry, he wouldn't bite. From now on, I'm the only one biting in here." And with that, he playfully bit her on her neck.

"Oooh," a slow, sensuous smile spread across Cory's face.

*

Being the man that he was, Adrian couldn't allow this opportunity to pass him by, after so many nights of fantasizing about her, all the while thinking about her, admiring her body, undressing her with his eyes, imagining what she would feel like. Now, he had her here in his shower, in his arms, finally. And if Adrian didn't have her now, he might as well explode. So if Cory thought he was going to back down from this one, she had another thought coming. She had teased him enough. He was done playing with her. If this was what she wanted, this was surely what she was going to get.

Adrian pulled her hard against him and kissed her. It was a slow but hungry kiss, as his tongue slipped inside her mouth exploring her sweetness. He wasn't in a hurry this time and warned himself to take it slow. And he had all the very best intentions but when her hot body pressed against his cool, naked one, his raw desire for her frightened even him.

He hastily pulled her T-shirt over her head and traced his fingers over the rise of her beautiful breasts. Adrian needed to taste her again, playfully nipping her as he went along. As he moved up her body, Cory gasped in delight against the tiled bathroom wall. Her shoulders were next, her neck, her earlobe and then back to her lips again.

Adrian hurriedly removed her tights. So much for taking it slow! Her matching pink bra and panties went next, quickly landing on the shower floor. Finally, he could see the beautiful body she hid under those power suits. Even his imagination had been way off. In an instant, he was on his knees, making circles with his tongue on her flat, naked stomach, his eyes taking their sweet time admiring her enticing Brazilian wax below.

"Nice job," Adrian murmured. He stopped and kissed her there, slowly. "No," he looked up at her and smiled. "*Really* nice."

*

"Um . . . glad you like it," Cory wobbled slightly when Adrian's heated kiss scorched her center. Thank God his big hands were firmly holding her slippery wet thighs still. The things this man could do to her, was doing to her, was just crazy. When he stood again, Adrian squirted shower gel into his hands and proceeded to lather her body with it.

Cory turned and leaned onto his strong chest for support and felt his hard-as-steel shaft pressing into her back. The small circular motions his hands made around her erect nipples sent her insane. Then his hands were moving all over her body, the firm movements massaging her flesh. Her shoulders, her stomach, her back, lower and lower. Adrian's wet and slippery hands together with the silky smoothness of the gel against her skin sent maddening, erotic sensations throughout her body. Sensations she believed she never experienced before now.

Adrian spun her around and finally lifted her around his waist, his hands comfortably kneading her fleshy behind. He turned the shower on again, his tongue and the water worked in unison to wash the soapy bubbles off her body.

"I want you, Cory," Adrian simply said to her. "And I don't think I ever wanted to make love to a woman as much as I want to right now. *Please* tell me you want this as much as I do."

"I do, Adrian. I want you to make love to me."

With Cory still sensually wrapped around him and both dripping from the shower, Adrian carried her into his bedroom. He grabbed a towel and began to dry her off as he sat on the bed.

Cory rested her uninjured leg on his thigh so that he had better access to her more intimate body parts. No man had ever done this to her before and it was driving her into euphoric ecstasy. She was shivering from the coolness of the bedroom but the feel of Adrian's hot tongue on her breast again instantly warmed her.

When he squeezed on her other breast, she felt the knots between her moist legs. Cory couldn't think straight, she could hardly breathe. One look from those mesmerizing eyes, one touch from those skilled hands and she was lost. Adrian kept her yearning for more with every sensuous stroke.

Cory climbed onto his muscular thighs now. One by one, Adrian took her nipples into his mouth, lightly licking them at first. Then he intensified the heat. Cory arched her back as Adrian sucked on her, her nails dug deeper into the hard flesh of his back.

Adrian's fingers lingered between her legs, gently massaging her sensitive flesh as moan after moan escaped her lips. Her skin hot and moist against his. Her engorged center felt the very same against his fingers inside her.

Cory closed her eyes and bit down hard on her lower lip, trying to conceal her cries. She wanted so much more of him but didn't know if her body could take such pleasure any longer.

"Adrian?" It was a soft but urgent sound, a half whisper and half moan coming from her.

"Yeah, baby?"

Cory, giddy from his lovemaking, announced, "Adrian, I have to tell you something. I haven't done this in a while."

"Really?" Adrian asked her, a bit shocked.

"With a man," she whispered.

Adrian immediately stopped everything he was doing to her and just stared at her. Now she had his undivided attention. "So . . . what exactly are we talking about here?" he asked smiling. "Are you into girls, then?"

"No! No! Of course not," Cory exclaimed. "It's just that after my last boyfriend I began using . . . um, toys instead."

"Toys?" he asked.

"Yes. Toys." Cory was waiting for him to explode into loud laughter but none came.

"I was never with a woman who was into toys before," Adrian

smiled. "Don't worry, though. I'll take real good care of you, baby."

When Adrian lifted her up, Cory instinctively wrapped her legs around his waist again, clinging to him for dear life.

"I promise," Adrian whispered to her.

Cory began kissing him hungrily, her moans becoming louder. Oh, she was definitely in the mood for some real loving now. "God, I want you so much, Adrian."

Adrian laid her on the bed and parted her thighs.

"Lord . . . you're so beautiful, Cory," Adrian whispered as he kissed her toes, then calves. He moved up to her succulent legs and thighs as she eagerly spread them wider for him. "And way too sumptuous."

Cory wasn't holding anything back. She was offering her sensuality to him on a silver platter. She could tell from his enlarged shaft just how much Adrian really wanted her and begged him to finally take her.

Adrian uttered a profanity when he entered Cory for the first time. "And oh so delicious," he moaned as he filled her.

Lying against the cool silkiness of his sheets, Cory felt his heat engulfing her body, scorching her all over. She begged for mercy when she felt Adrian's true power. He was moving in and out of her with an increased, but measured, intensity and strength as he plunged deeper and deeper into her opening.

"Work it for me, baby," Adrian urged her on as she gyrated to her own slow and sensual rhythm against every thrust.

Cory writhed in pure ecstasy, loving the feeling Adrian's every stroke was giving her. She delighted in every flick of his tongue and the maddening sensations his hot lips brought to her body. With every stroke, her subdued passion was awakened. She grabbed the bed sheets between her fingers and moaned out aloud her satisfaction.

That was when she flipped the script on him. She was now the one on top, riding him hard. Cory was so deliriously hot for this man right now. Now, she was really working it for him, erotically bouncing up and down his shaft.

"Cory . . . I don't think I could take this much longer if you keep that up, baby," Adrian breathlessly moaned.

"Just a little bit more, baby. Pleeeease," she cooed.

With her urging, Adrian rolled her over again, lifted her legs onto his shoulders this time and hammer-drilled even deeper into her, thrusting harder and faster.

"Ooohhh, yes!" Cory moaned. The man packed a serious hard-on, much better than any damn toy, any day. "Oh yeah, baby," a now-sweat drenched Cory begged Adrian to offer her body some release.

Adrian obliged. It didn't take long, as Cory screamed his name again and again. He grunted in pure pleasure as they exploded into each other, erotic spasms rocking their bodies.

She thought she knew what total and utter satisfaction was. Up until now, no man ever left her feeling so complete. Cory had to admit, this soldier could definitely handle the island heat. Her instincts were right on. Adrian Mendez was indeed an incredible lover. But even more incredible than she could have ever imagined.

"Oh my God. That was freaking amazing," an out-of-breath Cory was the first to admit as she lazily rolled on top of him again.

"No. That was much better than freaking amazing," Adrian grunted with labored breaths. He held her tightly around her waist so that she couldn't go anywhere. "But I don't think a word was invented yet to describe this," he laughed, still breathing heavily.

After his breathing slowed somewhat he said, "I was supposed to ask you something."

"Yeah? What's that?" Cory was eager to find out.

"When I called you today, I was going to ask you to have dinner with me tonight."

"Dinner?" Cory giggled. *That's right, usually the dinner came before the sex, Cory.*

"Yeah. Well, I figure I can still ask you although I assure you we'll be pretty busy for the remainder of tonight," he added, playing with her curls. "So Cory, would you like to have dinner with me on Friday night?"

Cory was in total amazement. After just making love to her, Adrian was asking her out to dinner? "Well, after what just happened here, how could I ever refuse you? Adrian, I'll love to have dinner with you on Friday night."

Adrian playfully rolled her over so that she was trapped under his lean body once more. "So are you hungry now?" he asked in a more serious tone.

Cory cupped his handsome face between her hands. Looking him straight in those beautiful brown eyes of his, she responded, "Only for you, baby."

"A very good answer," Adrian chuckled. "Well, I did warn you that we'll be real busy tonight." He spoke against her lips as he kissed her. "Cory," he paused, "the next time you plan on using your toys again, can I watch?"

"Sure." *If* she ever used them again.

When Cory felt Adrian's full arousal twitching and rubbing against her leg, she couldn't believe he was ready and raring to go again so soon. And she knew exactly why. Men and their avid fantasies. That was when she naughtily suggested, "But why wait? How 'bout I give you a little pre-show right now."

Chapter 14

Cory hobbled over to the elevator and prayed that she would make it through the rest of the day in one piece. She was in physical pain this morning. Besides her leg, all over her body ached. Maybe it wasn't such a good idea to have wild, wanton sex after such a long time. She felt like she had been through a military drill after trying all those positions with Adrian last night.

She inwardly groaned when she saw Jay already waiting for the lift. He was his flamboyant self in a lime green shirt and matching tie.

"Good morning, Ri-Ri. You look lovely this morning. All aglow," Jay announced in his usually disgusting and very chipper early morning tone. The caffeine junkie that he was always got his morning high from consuming way too much coffee. It was only 6:30 and the steaming cup he sipped from was already half empty and more than likely his second or third fix by now.

"Morning, Jay," she sang sweetly.

"Slept well?"

"Like a baby," Cory answered, smiling. Well, for the three hours she managed, anyway.

As she got into the elevator with him, he remarked, "You look shorter than usual this morning." Jay towered over her, his six foot four frame of lankiness looked down at her feet and saw flat sandals, instead of her usual heels. At five-five and wearing flats, Cory looked like a midget standing next to him.

"What's the matter with your foot, Ri-Ri?"

"Oh. I pulled a muscle jogging yesterday."

"Mmm. And judging from all those hickeys on your neck, you pulled other things, too," he grinned.

"God, Jay! Mind your own business," Cory said. Instinctively her hand flew to her neck.

"You slept with him, didn't you?"

"Leave me alone, Jay." Cory again prayed for the elevator to reach the fourth floor quickly enough so she could make her escape. Jay worked on the fifth floor with the big boys. The chairman, CEO, CFO and finance department were all located there. Thank God it finally stopped on her floor and she hobbled out again.

"So how was it?" he shouted after her.

"In-freaking-credible!" Cory threw back at him. Knowing Jay for so long, only a retort like that would leave him completely satisfied. He was laughing hard when the elevator door closed.

Cory grinned herself. It was the truth. She did find out something last night. What an absolutely amazing lover Adrian was. And after assessing her fair share of sexual relationships, he was by far the best she ever had. The lieutenant was right at the top of her list. His sexual prowess made her spirit soar to new heights, orgasm after orgasm, sending her to the edge and back. She truly lost count of the many screaming ones she experienced last night.

Forget about the battery-operated stuff, where had this man been all her life? It couldn't get better than the real thing Adrian delivered. This was the only time she ever allowed a man to take total possession of her entire being like that. And he certainly had no qualms about pleasing a woman in his bed. Adrian made her do things she never dreamt of. She had become totally enslaved in his passion last night. And how was it possible that she still yearned for him this morning when she awoke, alone in her own bed? Cory couldn't quite get enough, the fire, the heat and that burning desire for him. And she wanted so much more of it.

*

And that was exactly what she got for the next couple of weeks. For the first time in a long time, she felt happy. After all she had been through, Cory truly felt like she was living again. She felt free. Adrian Mendez freed her soul from the grasps of hell. And with each passing day, it became even more magical.

The only problem was . . . it was starting to be more than sex she wanted from Adrian.

She was falling for Adrian . . . and fast. How could she really resist him? On the outside, Adrian was gorgeous, sexy, and physically fit. On the inside he was kind, caring, intelligent, respected her modern femininity, very protective of her, and appreciated her for who she was really.

There was only one problem. This incredible package came all wrapped up in a military uniform. With the guns and ammunition included. The man killed people for a living. Could she really be with someone like Adrian?

And she had no idea of his feelings for her. He certainly never said anything to her to ever suggest he wanted more than sex from her.

She was busy packing for her upcoming Carnival weekend getaway trip with her family when she realized she needed to talk it over with a friend. And Cory knew her friends well so she couldn't possibly call Gabby. Gabby was the girlfriend for those hardcore, ugly truth talks. She'd call Kerry if she needed a psychoanalysis of something. When she was in the mood for a hilarious, laugh-out-loud perspective, she'd consult Jay. So she dialed Elisha's number.

"Hola, chica! Como esta?"

"Ah, she speaks Spanish. That means she's in a good mood," Elisha laughed. "So does this have anything to do with soldier boy?"

"Oh yeah. It has everything to do with him. These past few weeks have been just amazing. I've not been this happy in so long."

"I know. Well, I'm just so happy to see you happy and actually living again, Cory."

"But I think I'm falling for him, Ellie," Cory blurted. "Really hard."

"Hold up. Are you saying you're falling in love with Adrian?" Elisha asked.

There was a long silence before Cory finally answered her. "I think I might be."

"Okay." Pause. "So how does Adrian feel about all this?"

"I don't know, Ellie. I really don't know. I mean I know he likes me, we spend a lot of time together and we really enjoy each other's company and the sex is just so damn good . . . but I don't know much else. He hasn't said anything to indicate his feelings in that department."

"Oh. I see."

"After Preston, I never thought I could feel this way again. In fact, Preston can't even compare to Adrian. Adrian is so different. He knows what I need and he's not afraid to give it to me. He's kind and patient and humble. And he's so protective of me all the time. He even introduced me to new things."

"New things like what?"

"Like hiking through the bush."

"No! Way! You hiking, Cory?" Elisha burst out laughing. "That's something I have to see for myself. Wait till Gabby and Kerry hear this."

"Don't laugh. It's actually fun. You all should come with our group sometime," Cory suggested.

"Uh-huh, sure," Elisha continued laughing. "I could see Kerry now, in her matching hiking gear."

"By the way, how's she and Gabs doing? I haven't seen them both in a while. I called Kerry sometime but she never returned my call. I thought that was odd."

"Well, you know Gabs is busy finishing up her culinary degree. And as for Kerry . . . I think you two need to talk."

"Talk? About what?" Cory enquired.

"Well, I think since that time you introduced us to Adrian at that party . . . she kinda felt you were being a—"

"A what? A hypocrite?" Cory asked defensively. "Does Kerry think I'm a hypocrite, Elisha?"

"Look, I didn't say that. I think she was probably hurt by your whole antimilitary thing the whole time. Remember her brother is a cop?"

"I know that. It's not like I don't like him or anything. I do. Besides, I'm not like that anymore. At least, I'm trying to change my way of thinking, Elisha. And I have to thank Adrian for that."

"Well, whatever it is, you and Kerry have to work it out between yourselves," Elisha proclaimed. "Anyway, let's get back to your dilemma."

"Okay, so you tell me this," Cory said. "What do you call two people who spend every other day together, who go out with each other, who have so much fun together. . ."

"Wait a minute. You two actually *leave* his apartment?" Elisha laughed.

"Could you stop interrupting me here? And yes, we do go out. Sometimes," Cory laughed. "And . . . . we have the most incredible sex ever. Remember when I joked and told you all I needed four men to completely satisfy me?

"Yeah."

"Well, Ellie . . . I only need half of that man. Okay. *Only half!*"

"Really?" Elisha squealed. "Damn girl, I knew soldier boy was hot."

"So what exactly do you call us, Ellie? Are we dating, are we a couple? What are we?"

"Sex buddies!"

"I was afraid you were going to say that," Cory sighed.

"But wasn't that what you wanted to begin with? You wanted him just for the sex, remember?"

"Yeah, I did," Cory muttered.

"And now you want more, don't you?"

"Oh, Ellie. I want so much more. And I want it all with him."

"Girl, you got it bad. It sounds like you're hooked all right."

"Ellie, I need some help here, please."

"Cory, all I can tell you is to ask him how he feels about you. Or you tell him how you feel about him."

"Are you crazy? I can't do that."

"What's the matter with you? You always go after what you want."

"Yeah, but this is different. He's different."

"Look, sometimes men just need a little prodding and prompting. Maybe he's a little shy to admit his feelings just yet."

"Yeah, maybe you're right." Cory doubted it was that, though. "Did you ever have to prod and prompt Curtis?"

"Of course I had to!"

Cory laughed. "Of course. What am I asking? Men will be men. Anyways, I have to get back to my packing. So enjoy the Carnival. I'll call you over the weekend."

"And you enjoy the beach."

Cory groaned aloud. She didn't exactly want to be stuck at a beach house this weekend, especially since all her friends would be playing mas' without her, again. But if you weren't a masquerader or spectator during the Carnival festivities, the beach was usually your domain.

By the time she was finished packing, Cory knew she had to find out where things stood between her and Adrian. And soon. Some way or the other. So maybe she really needed to start the prodding and prompting.

Chapter 15

Finally, the extra two-day-long weekend everyone on the island was eagerly anticipating arrived in mid-February. When the euphoria that was Trinidad and Tobago's Carnival finally climaxed into the two days of magical revelry, Adrian was quite happy to be back as a costumed masquerader again, dancing through the streets—"playing mas" as the locals said. He had missed this colorful spectacle and he missed the intense heat of the sun beating down his back as he danced under it.

It wasn't dubbed the greatest show on earth for nothing. Introduced to the island by French settlers, Carnival was one of the biggest street parties in the world and by far Adrian's favorite national festival here. The West Indian Labor Day Parade he attended growing up in Brooklyn got its impetus from this one. Only, Trinidad's Carnival was a hundred times better in his book. In fact, no other Carnivals could compare to it in the world, Adrian thought. It was the creativity and passion of the people put on display here.

Most importantly, Carnival was all about the women, especially since they were some of the most beautiful on the planet. Their pretty made-up faces, sexy bikini-and-beads-clad bodies, along with their gyrating waistlines swaying in sweet abandon on the streets, undoubtedly made them his main ingredient. They came in all varied shapes and shades but how they loved to tease and entice their male counterparts. They were just as spicy as the food served up on the island.

Maybe that got to him because whilst in the band, completely surrounded by beautiful, sensuous women, Adrian found himself thinking of one particular naughty hottie. For the first time he realized something was missing for him. And just like the Carnival Jumbie roaming the island, its weary spirit stalking the inhabitants, Cory's charms were becoming harder for him to resist day by day. There was something about Cory that was getting under his skin and her warmth was melting his heart. Her beautiful eyes, infectious laughter, and sweet smile. Adrian was missing her.

Not good! Wasn't he supposed to keep her at arm's length, just like the rest of them? Just a quick roll in the sack until they were both completely satisfied? But Adrian seriously doubted his ability to have his fill and then let go of her. Ever since the first time they had made love, Adrian still couldn't get over that sexy little pre-show Cory gave him. Would he really be able to let Cory go after that?

The more he had her, the more he wanted. How could he ever get enough of those beautiful legs wrapped around him or those succulent nipples instantly hardening against his tongue? Erotic thoughts immediately conjured in his mind of the things he would have been doing to her, if only she was here with him now.

However, these were not possible as Cory was miles away, spending the Carnival weekend with her family in Mayaro. This little seaside fishing village was all the way down on the southeastern side of the island and he was in the northwest. They were at two completely opposite ends of the spectrum but Adrian felt like he had to at least hear her voice to ease this ache.

*

Since Cory was stuck at a beach house with about twenty of her relatives for the long weekend, when she answered her cell phone, she immediately began, "Well, I hope you're having a rotten time playing in the band without me."

The rented house was filled with people and way too noisy for her liking. She hadn't wanted to come but they had been planning this for almost a year. It was supposed to be a family weekend getaway to celebrate her father's sixtieth birthday. It was what he had wanted. It meant she was away from Adrian going on four days now and the longest time they were apart from each other.

Adrian had to practically shout through his cell phone so that Cory could hear him. "Is that the kind of greeting I'm going to get from my girl?" he asked.

"I'm sure there are thousands of girls around to hold your interests."

"You may think so but why am I calling you, then?"

"I don't know, maybe because you're missing me like crazy?"

"God, Cory . . . I miss you so much right now. I wish you were here with me."

"Yeah? I don't have a costume, remember?"

"Oh, I wasn't talking about playing in the band with me," Adrian teased.

"Then what're you talking about?" She knew very well but needed to hear him say just how much he wanted her.

"Well, I'll give you a hint. It has to do with me and playing with you but not in the band."

"Adrian!" Cory cried. "What're you saying?"

"I'm saying I want you so much right now, Cory."

It was more like a seductive whisper, sending warmth throughout her entire body.

Adrian hesitated before he asked, "Cory . . . could you get up here to the city today?"

After only briefly contemplating his offer, Cory's mind was made. Of course she could get to Port of Spain today.

"And Cory, please be careful," was the last thing she had heard Adrian say before she ended the conversation.

She had planned to leave the village soon anyway to head back home. She now had new plans. It meant she would have to endure a longer drive to Adrian's apartment instead. Alone. Cory quickly packed her stuff and said a quick goodbye to her relatives.

Her father was a bit suspicious of her decision to head out earlier but he didn't say anything. Anytime he pulled his glasses lower down his nose bridge, it signaled his speculative moments.

She used the excuse of wanting to catch a glimpse of the Carnival parade in the city after all. Cory hadn't yet introduced Adrian to him because she wasn't sure where they were heading, if anywhere at all.

It was now a little after one on Carnival Tuesday afternoon. If she was lucky, she should be seeing Adrian anywhere around three. Cory drove cautiously but with a purpose. She had to be extra careful with the winding roads in this part of the island.

With the radio on, her windows down and the wind blowing through her hair, Cory concentrated on the things she was going to do to that man when she saw him. With eager anticipation, her foot hit the gas pedal harder with every new erotic thought.

As she drove to the city, the island's changing landscape dramatically transformed before her eyes. From the coconut tree-lined coasts, to the greenery of the rural villages she passed, to the long stretch of highway and eventually to the modern high-rise glass structures punctuating the Caribbean city.

After almost running over a herd of goats and zipping through a few amber lights, she finally made it in one piece. It seemed like she drove and drove and drove. Luckily, the roads were clear of all traffic as many people were either in the city looking at or masquerading today. Cory made sure she kept on the outskirts of the city as the interior would have undoubtedly become impenetrable with masqueraders, spectators, vendors and the many huge music trucks snaking their way through the crowded streets.

Approximately one hour and forty-five minutes later, she pulled up in front of Adrian's apartment building. *The things people do for sex.*

*

When Adrian had told his cousins he was heading home after complaining about the sun being too hot today, they all knew he was lying. At the moment, he didn't really care what they thought. Luckily, his band had reached a close twenty minutes walking distance to his place. Getting a taxi anywhere here in this chaos was impossible, so he had to foot it. Walking home wasn't that bad either once thoughts of Cory were in his head. They were the only motivation he needed.

Already runaway beads and other remnants of discarded costumes lay strewn about the streets. Varying hues of brightly colored materials in golds and oranges, blues and greens dazzled in the midday sun. Adrian headed straight for the shower. He had to scrub himself extra hard to get rid of all the glitter on his chest. He had immaculate timing because as he was drying off, he heard his doorbell chiming.

"What the hell . . . " he muttered and instinctively glanced at his watch.

When he answered the door, clad in only a plush navy blue towel wrapped seductively low around his waist, an impatient Cory was waiting.

"I thought you said two-and-a-half hours. What, did you fly?" he chided. "God, Cory . . . I asked you to be careful."

"But I did. I'm here in one piece, aren't I?" an indignant Cory responded. "Look, Adrian, I sure as hell didn't drive all the way here to argue with you, okay?"

Adrian didn't mean to sound so harsh with her but if anything had happened to her, he didn't know what he would have done. He was feeling pretty guilty after his phone call. He was the selfish one who wanted her so badly that he asked her to drive all the way down here.

Adrian softened with a smile. "Oh, yeah. So what exactly did you come here for, then?" He didn't really give Cory a chance to answer as he pulled her inside and kissed her fiercely. This was what he was really missing in the band. Cory in his arms.

"You look delicious, baby," Adrian crooned as he nibbled her ear. "I really missed you this weekend." There, he said it.

*

Adrian's skin, still damp from his shower, rubbed against her hot flesh. "Now that's more like it," Cory laughed as she took him all in. This man was just too damn gorgeous for his own good. There were still remnants of gold glitter dust on his rippled chest, evidence that he was indeed a Carnival masquerader. It added to the golden sparkle in his eyes. And he smelled so intoxicatingly masculine.

Adrian locked the front door behind her. Cory backed against it for support. Her body's temperature was soaring, so hot. But she knew it wasn't entirely from the heat outside—it was more from all those erotic thoughts she'd conjured in her mind during the long drive over.

The anticipation Cory found to be highly intoxicating in itself. She was already wet and giddy with desire for him. She tipped on her toes, throwing her arms around his neck. In an instant, Adrian's delicious mouth was all over hers again. Cory didn't even realize when her handbag and car keys slipped through her hands and landed on the floor. Finally, she could have him at last.

"So, what do you have under there for me?" she cooed. Cory gently tugged at the towel and allowed it to fall to the gleaming wooden floor. Now there was no barrier depriving her from having him right there. The view of Adrian's well-defined torso and hard erection generated an intense sensation from her already hard clit.

"Now, to answer your question." She took his huge erection into her hands, stroking him. "This is what I really came here for."

Adrian moaned. His deep, animal-like sound that sent her all shivery. "You know I'm surely gonna make your long drive here worth it, right baby?"

"Uh-huh," Cory answered him eagerly. Still, this wasn't enough for her. She needed to hear the real effect she had on him. Just like the kind he had on her. Lawyers and accountants were the usual men she went out with. Now, here was this second lieutenant she couldn't seem to get enough of. No man before seemed to rock her world quite like Adrian. In fact, no man could cause her to drive all the way from Mayaro to Port of Spain for almost two hours, just for this.

Armed with a wicked grin on her face, Cory knelt in the foyer. Her hand tightly encircled him as she teased the tip of his shaft with her wet tongue. Gently, she began to lick him like her favorite ice cream cone. First the tip and then all along his entire length.

Adrian shuddered. Then his breath became ragged. He inhaled sharply.

"Oooh . . . God, Cory."

Oh yeah, that's what I want to hear, baby. Cory covered him with her lips then, reaching down as far as her throat would allow, sucking on him.

Adrian tugged at her wild curls. "God, baby . . . what're you doing to me?" he whispered in his utterly raspy but sexy voice she loved.

Cory stopped for a few seconds to reply, "Only what you do to me, baby."

Adrian pulled her up. "As much as I'm liking this right now, I think I'll pass on the foreplay. Just for now, okay, baby." He began to unzip her shorts. "Because I need you now, Cory. I need to show you how much I missed you." But the snug pair of faded denim shorts wasn't budging off her wide hips. "Baby, how did you get into this thing?"

Cory giggled as she tried to wiggle her way out the fitted material. "I only wore it with you in mind, you know."

"That's totally not necessary. You could show up here in a brown paper bag for all I care."

"Oh, really?"

"Here's the deal. I'll go get the latex, you figure your way out of those," Adrian said but with an urgency in his voice.

He made a Usain Bolt-Olympic-gold-medal-dash into his bedroom. "Fine. I don't need your help," she shouted after him.

Cory reveled in the ways Adrian reacted to her body and to her sexual whims and fancies. He had absolutely no problems showing his feelings for her where that was concerned. The problem apparently lay with the spoken word. He just hadn't said anything to her as yet that indicated his feelings for her.

By the time she did get her shorts off Adrian was back, latex perfectly intact. Cory was completely naked too, posing provocatively against the door.

"Why're you still all the way over there?" Adrian asked, a puzzled look on his face.

"Because I want you to do me right here."

Adrian laughed. "Oh, you know I'll do you anywhere, anytime you like, baby. Right now, there's nothing better I'd rather see than the look on your face when you cum for me, Cory."

Now it was Adrian's turn to get down on his knees. Lifting one sexy leg over his shoulders he began to have her for lunch, kissing her erotic center long and hard.

Cory bucked from the feel of his warm lips on hers. It was a sensuous kiss, his hot slippery tongue sliding in and out of her throbbing and swollen clit.

"Ooh . . . my . . . " Cory said, not quite sure what the hell she wanted to say at the moment. One hand glued Adrian's head to her center, the other furiously scratched at the front door like a wild animal trying to get out. This was just what her body had been craving these last four days. Just what the doctor ordered. Not having Adrian all those days was just torturous for her soul.

Adrian feverishly and hungrily seduced her with his tongue, penetrating her with it. Delving into her. Devouring her.

Not that Cory wanted him to ever move from that erotic spot anytime soon but she felt like she just couldn't take this for much longer. In fact, she was too close to having her first orgasm in four days. With every sweet lick of his tongue, she tipped higher on her toes, trembling and shaking. Adrian remained on spot to finish the job he started, staying there long enough for her to enjoy her first one. Cory exhaled huge breaths of air as her body shuddered as she came.

"So how was your lunch, LT?" a breathless Cory asked.

"Mmmm, like honey, baby," Adrian answered, licking his already wet lips.

That was all the answer she needed. Adrian positioned her to face the door. Without having to say anything, Cory eagerly spread her legs apart for him.

"Am I under arrest?" she giggled.

"Only if you want to be," Adrian slid some damp strands behind her ear and planted a kiss on her shoulder.

"Nah. I know you want me too much right now. It's my turn to pleasure you, baby."

Wanting him to wait no more, Cory seductively gyrated her hips allowing him to ease his throbbing shaft into her from behind, slowly at first, her tight muscles gripping his hard-as-steel manhood for dear life.

"Mmmm," she moaned. Adrian nibbled on her neck while he caressed her hardened nipples.

"So tell me, Cory," he spoke directly into her ear. "Is *this* what you really came all the way here for?" Adrian rammed further into her, indicating the exact answer he required from her.

"Oh, Adrian. *Yes!*" Cory exclaimed with a gut-wrenching moan, angling her body, taking every measured and intensified stroke Adrian delivered. His sinfully sweet thrusts plunging deeper, harder . . . faster now with every powerful stroke, massaging her fleshy behind.

"Thought so." Her arms were pressed up against the door, now rattling madly on its hinges. Between her loud moans and Adrian's deep grunts every time he withdrew and slammed into her again and the rattling door, it crossed Cory's mind that anyone passing in the corridor might think somebody was being murdered up in here. She still couldn't care less what anyone might be thinking right now. That was the effect Adrian's love-making had on her. She became liberated. She only felt sweet ecstasy anytime this man was inside her.

Together with the pulsating soca beats breezily floating through Adrian's apartment from outside, the two lovers became entrapped in their own Carnival rhythm. By the time Cory climaxed again, Adrian had her in a position of counting her ten beautifully polished toes as he enjoyed listening to her come in Spanish this time. Cory never before came this hard. When it was his turn, Adrian did his in English. Dirty American-English to be exact. And his door stood up to the battering of its life. It could withstand a category five hurricane obviously.

*

"Are you okay, baby?" Adrian asked, carrying Cory's limp body over to the sofa. He was trying to catch his breath as he laid her down on the sofa. Since her last explosive foreign climax, she hadn't said a word.

When he looked into her eyes, there were tears glistening.

"Cory, did I hurt you just now? What is it?" Adrian asked her frantically. Maybe he had been a bit too rough and heavy with her this time. He was just so damn excited to see her today.

The crazy sensations this woman's body stirred in him. Those agonizingly, sinfully sweet sensations that rocked and jolted his body every time she spread her legs to have him. In fact, the mere sight of her could stir such sensations. Then feeling her. Pleasuring her body with his. It was just crazy the way her body responded to his every touch. Cory could boost any man's ego in that department. Adrian prayed to God he hadn't hurt her just now.

"No, I'm fine," she answered.

Adrian breathed a sigh of relief. "Then tell me, why're you crying, baby?"

"No!" she blurted out.

"Cory, c'mon." Adrian prodded some more but she wasn't budging. Just when he was about to drop it, she finally opened up to him.

"It's just that . . . I'm in love with you, Adrian."

Chapter 16

Love? Cory was in love with him? Never in a million years had Adrian expected to hear these words. He never saw this one coming. And especially from Cory! He figured a woman like her only needed a man like him for one thing. He thought some good loving was all she had wanted. And he was only more than willing to give it to her for as long as she needed it. Adrian knew she could never complain about him handling his business with her because he definitely left her more than satisfied on every occasion. She didn't need those toys anymore, for damn sure.

Then his long, stunned male silence kicked in. What more could she possibly want with him? Cory made it quite clear what she thought of military men since the first day they officially met. When did love become a part of her agenda? Now Adrian was really confused. He was at a complete loss for words and the deafening silence grew even longer in the room.

His mind was working like clockwork trying to decipher everything that just happened here. Adrian hadn't even noticed their relationship's course changing. Did they even have a relationship? And if they did, what was the basis of it? Sure they were lovers, they went out together, enjoyed each other's company. Cory was definitely the only woman in his life. The only woman he shared his bed with. But he had been so intent on protecting his shattered heart for so long now that he wasn't one hundred percent ready to confront his true feelings for Cory.

Yes, Cory was undeniably beautiful, insanely fantastic in bed, she could also be a little nutty sometimes but Adrian loved that about her. He loved spending time with her; being around her was food for his starving soul. Her laughter, music for it to dance. But he just wasn't sure he was in love.

*

Cory wished he would just say something. Anything. But nothing came. Now what did she do? Shouting her feelings like some crazy school girl? And why was she feeling like she just made a complete fool of herself in the process?

One moment the man had her coming in Spanish and touching her ten toes for the love of it which no man has ever caused her to do before. What next? A black leather outfit and a whip? Or fish nets and stilettos? Then in another instant, she was blurting out feelings of love for the man. Why couldn't she just keep her mouth shut? Ha! So much for Elisha's stupid advice.

Finally, Cory gave into the fact that this conversation was going nowhere. She got up to go to the kitchen wearing nothing but her shattered pride. Wishing to forget the folly she'd just uttered, she asked him nonchalantly, "Do you have anything to drink in your refrigerator?"

Again, Adrian didn't even bother to answer her. He was still at a loss for words it seemed. Maybe he hadn't heard her. And hopefully, any of the other foolishness she just uttered, too.

*

But Adrian had heard all right. The last thing he wanted to do in this world was to hurt Cory. Thoughts of Natacha began flooding his mind then. Was he afraid to admit his feelings now because of what he had gone through with her?

Over the years and because of this he had mastered the art of masking his true feelings so well. He had even gotten the crazy idea to tattoo a cobra over his heart for protection. But the truth was, he didn't feel anything where Natacha was concerned anymore. He had Cory to thank for that. He had her now. In his life. In his bed. And in his heart. She made all that pain go away. *So why can't you just tell her that, fool?*

Adrian lay on the sofa totally satiated but still stared into oblivion. In his mind he recalled a previous opportunity he had to tell Cory his feelings. But he had chickened out then, too. They were having dinner at a restaurant on the western peninsula one night.

Adrian loved this area, it was so quiet and serene. He had spent a lot of time training through the heavy forested area and had been hiking there many times, as well as going on many shooting expeditions, too. The lush greenness of the vegetation and the quiet charm and calm this area offered made it one of his favorite places on the island.

Adrian remembered that night well. Cory was wearing an elegant turquoise-colored maxi dress. He distinctively remembered her outfit because it was the first time he had seen her wearing anything past her knees. She had looked so beautiful, her hair falling wildly about her shoulders. In fact, she always looked beautiful to him. Adrian loved her wild messy hair, it was what made Cory . . . well, Cory. He loved it even more when they made love and it became a tangled mess, clinging to her sweaty shoulders.

The restaurant had offered outdoor dining under the warm Caribbean star-filled night. It was quite a lovely picture with the anchored yachts bobbing on the calm sea and the lights of the city in the distance twinkling behind them.

"This is really beautiful. Adrian, I love it here," Cory had remarked about the restaurant. It was the beauty and the history of the place she had appreciated, since the area was settled by an indigenous Arawak Indian tribe who gave the area its name, Chaguaramas.

When the waitress had brought their orders over, Cory immediately attacked her plate of succulent shrimp in a coconut curry sauce. He'd chosen the lobster tails in lime butter.

"Baby, this is sooo good," Cory broke out into her orgasmic-like moaning. "You have to try this." She stuck one juicy shrimp on her fork and fed it to Adrian. His face immediately turned a dark red color.

"Oh, hot. Hot," he complained. He literally felt like hot steam coming through his ears. "Cory, why's that so spicy?" Adrian began coughing now. "How could you eat that stuff?" More coughs.

"It's not that hot," Cory laughed as he swallowed several gulps of the water on the table, trying to cool his mouth. "You know I like my food spicy," she offered.

Tears were forming in his eyes.

"Adrian, are you, okay?" Cory asked sounding both concerned and guilty.

"Yeah, I'm good," he coughed some more. "But please, no more hot peppers, baby. You know I like my woman spicy. Not my food, okay."

"Okay," she smiled wickedly. "I'll keep that in mind when we get home."

When things had cooled down after dinner, they watched the yachts and took in the sheer ambiance of the place and each other. That was when Cory sprung her list of requirements on him. These were supposedly her terms of what people should expect from each other.

"Oh, boy," he had silently groaned. He'd wondered where Cory was heading with all this when she boldly proceeded to list her requirements. He should have figured out her feelings for him then.

"Honesty is at the top of the list," she began. "Then there is faithfulness and respect." And she went on and on. By the time she had listed about fifteen of her requirements, Adrian's head was spinning.

"Whoa, that sure is a long list, Cory," he responded.

"It's not so long," she protested.

"Do you mind if I ask you where you got this crazy idea for a list of requirements, anyway?"

"From a book by Steve Harvey," she replied nonchalantly.

"Steve Harvey?" Adrian asked incredulously. He started grinning then.

"What?" Cory shot back at him.

Adrian was in stitches, laughing. "Cory, just in case you didn't realize, the guy's a comedian. And here you are taking love advice from the man?"

"Hey, that was a really good book. It was a bestseller, too. It was so funny and it did have a lot of helpful information, just so you know," Cory interjected.

Adrian didn't get women. They were willing to read anything and take it as the gospel. Books, magazines, articles. For instance, they'd read how to lose weight, how to spice up their love life, and what kind of man they should marry and believe the crap. From the time a real man pours out his true feelings to them and tells them he loves them, what do they do? They shut him down, walk away, or never believe the brotha. That was why he wasn't about to head down that road again.

"So what are your requirements then, Adrian?"

"My requirement is that you don't have so many requirements," he joked.

"Adrian, come on, this is important. Stop playing."

"Cory, first of all I think you have way too many requirements." If she wrote it down, the thing would have probably resembled a grocery list, Adrian thought. "But on a serious note and if you must know, my one and only requirement is that you understand what I do as a soldier and respect it. You don't have to like it. Just respect it, Cory."

"*That's it?* You have one requirement?"

"One requirement," Adrian maintained.

"Are you sure? Not cook your meals? Do your laundry?"

"Nope, none of that stuff is required."

"Well, I think I may be able to work with that," she had smiled.

But Adrian didn't know if Cory was quite prepared to do that just yet. If she ever could accept that fact and understand the responsibilities that came along with it. He knew that had been his major reason for not telling her how absolutely crazy he was about her. But in the following weeks Adrian did notice her overcoming this. Now, he still couldn't tell her.

*

Since he wasn't even looking at her, Cory pressed her hot forehead against the cool, gleaming stainless steel of Adrian's refrigerator door. She chided herself silently. She realized it was high time she separate the sex from the love like him. She had to start taking Steve's advice and start thinking like a man. Adrian's stunned silence alone signified that his interests were purely sexual in nature. He was a man, after all. No, he was a *military* man, she reminded herself. And this was all he needed from her.

When she returned to the sofa, drink in hand, she was a totally different person. She was back to her cheery self again.

"Do you want a drink, baby?" she cooed sweetly. Adrian shook his head in refusal. Cory seductively pouted her lips. "Do you want some of me instead, then?" she asked playfully.

Adrian smiled. "Now, when have I ever refused you?"

"Never!"

"Hmmm, and I wonder why that is? Come here, baby," he spoke softly. Adrian kissed her so tenderly then.

Yes, I wonder that myself sometimes, Adrian. That's it, Cory. Think like a man. Act like a lady. And screw him till he's senseless.

Chapter 17

It was Adrian's turn to go to the refrigerator. After making love to Cory all afternoon long, he was ravenous. And after performing like that, a man had to eat to keep his strength up. He took two frozen pasta meals from the freezer and popped one into the microwave.

A single guy living the bachelor lifestyle really didn't have much choice when it came to eating. Though he lived on an island that abounded with fresh produce, seafood, and poultry he still ate out a lot, feasted on fast food, or had tons of frozen meals on hand. He wasn't much of a chef either. Mac 'n' cheese was his best friend as far as actually cooking a meal went.

He stood next to the microwave drumming his fingers on the countertop, waiting for the beep. Meals like this often reminded him of the ones he had when he was out in the field back in Afghanistan. Adrian remembered the many steaming meals of rice and beans he had for dinner in those days. This also reminded him of how happy he was to be back in Trinidad. Especially since he had Cory now, a sensuous and beautiful woman who was in love with him.

Adrian forgot his thoughts and turned toward the door when he heard a key turning in it. Anna-Marie? What a swell time for his sister to show up here, Adrian groaned. Damn, he had forgotten all about her and that extra key. Anna-Marie entered the apartment then, still dressed in her Carnival costume, well, what was left of it, anyway.

"Hey, bro, what're you doing home already?" Anna beamed at him.

"Um, I think I live here, Anna," Adrian replied.

"I know that. You know what I mean." Anna came over and gave him a peck on the cheek. "I thought you'd still be out partying till midnight or something."

"Actually, I left the band earlier this afternoon."

"*What?* Why would you do that, Adrian?" At that exact moment, Cory chose to emerge from Adrian's bedroom. "Baby, don't forget to open the bottle of wine for me," she announced.

A knowing smile immediately replaced Anna's dropped jaw. "Well, hello," Anna said to Cory.

*

Cory hadn't seen the woman standing there.

"Oh my God!" Cory exclaimed as she spun around to face the voice. It had an American accent, just like Adrian's. "You scared me. I'm so sorry, I thought we were alone." Thank God she was actually wearing clothes now.

"Not anymore," Adrian joked. "Cory this is my sister, Anna-Marie. Anna this is Cory."

After my whole admission thing this afternoon, I'm still just Cory.

"Oh, hi, Anna-Marie, it's a pleasure to finally meet you," Cory said. "Adrian speaks of you all the time."

"I do?" Adrian asked, feigning stupidity.

"Please, call me Anna," Anna-Marie offered. She turned to Adrian and remarked, "So I see you've been pretty busy, bro. Are you keeping things from your big sister now?" There was a hint of mischief in her voice, not to mention the big grin filling her face.

"That's because I don't want you all up in my business, Anna," Adrian teased. "So what brings you by, anyway?"

"I thought I'd swing by to rest my aching feet a while till the after-Carnival traffic clears up. I certainly didn't expect you to be home so early. *And* with company."

"So how was your Carnival?" Cory asked Anna.

"Oh, fantastic! I had a great time playing this year."

"Now I really feel like I'm the only one who didn't play," Cory said.

"Don't you worry. There's always next year," Anna said.

"Yeah, that's for sure," Cory cheered up. "I love your costume by the way," she added, admiring the white two-piece bikini clad on Anna's svelte body. It was heavily beaded with crystals and rhinestones hanging from it and completed with a beautiful white and silver feathered head-piece Anna was holding in her hands.

"Thank you, Cory."

Cory noticed the resemblance between Anna and Adrian, too. She had the same light brown complexion as his, only hers was more pale and porcelain-looking against her straight black hair that was upswept in a ponytail. Anna was taller than her and much more slender. She was also a very busty girl for someone so slim. The bikini top of her costume was obviously straining.

Anna certainly didn't look like a woman who had two young boys, though. And which man in their right thinking mind would want to divorce her anyway? Cory wondered. She was so beautiful. Cory immediately hated the jerk. Whoever he was.

The microwave beeped. "Do you want some dinner, sis?" Adrian asked as he popped another meal into the microwave. "It's nothing fancy but it'll fill you up."

"I'd love to stay for dinner with you guys," Anna beamed.

"Since when're you so excited about food? You hardly ever eat anything."

"I'm starving, that's all," she grinned.

"Well, we have from the box grilled Chicken Alfredo with broccoli and some wine for us to wash it all down with," Cory said.

"That sounds wonderful to me, Cory."

Cory laughed. She had immediately taken a liking to Anna. She was warm and friendly. She knew they would become good friends. If Adrian ever told her how he really felt about her. Memories of his deafening silence earlier on in the afternoon came to mind but Cory quickly snuffed them out. There was no reason to dampen her mood again.

Anna helped Cory set the dining table for three while Adrian continued to man the microwave. Cory took the salad she made out of the refrigerator along with the bottle of Merlot Adrian uncorked for her.

"So, Cory, it looks like we have a lot of catching up to do," Anna announced as she touched Cory lightly on the arm.

Adrian rolled his eyes heavenward.

"Yes, we do," Cory replied. "So what do you do, Anna?"

"Well, when I'm not chasing around my two boys, or looking out for my little brother, I read the news on television."

"Oh, my God! I knew it. You're that news anchor. The one on the government channel. No wonder your face looked so familiar," Cory exclaimed.

"And since when do you look at the news?" Adrian interjected from the kitchen.

"Since recently."

The three of them sat at the table and began to eat their modest dinner. The sounds of knives and forks scraped against the plates as they ate.

"Ooh, I knew I came by for another reason," Anna interrupted the silence.

"Besides to snoop around?" Adrian grinned.

"I wanted to remind you of Aunty Claudia's anniversary party on Saturday."

"Damn, that's this Saturday?" Adrian asked.

"Yes, it is, Adrian. And don't tell me you forgot or you have to work."

"No, I'm available. I just forgot the date, that's all."

"Well, I can see you have *other* things going on in your life now, so I'll forgive you."

"Gee, thanks," Adrian said dryly.

It was very easy for Cory to notice the love these two siblings had for each other, even amidst the rivalry. She knew how much

Adrian cared for his family. And she only now discovered just how protective Anna was over Adrian, even though he was a grown-ass man. It reminded her so much of she and Collin. God, she missed him so much.

"So you can bring Cory, then. And introduce her to the entire Mendez clan," Anna happily added.

Only briefly, a look of absolute horror flashed across Adrian's face.

"That's a great idea," he smiled at Cory but sounded a bit shaky. "So, I hope you have dancing shoes, baby."

"Oh, shoes I have," Cory answered cheerfully. Adrian would find out sooner or later about her little shoe fetish. Okay, maybe it was more like a shoe obsession but she just loved shoes.

"And does this also mean that you want your keys back, too?" Anna laughed again.

Adrian was serious, "That'll be nice. Lord knows I don't need you bouncing up in here, seeing things you shouldn't be seeing."

Anna and Cory burst out laughing. "Don't worry, bro, you look like you're in very good hands now," Anna said. "Maybe you can give them to Cory now."

Cory's attention immediately snapped back to Anna and what she was saying.

"That's a great idea," Adrian responded in pretty much the same tone as before.

Cory looked at him in surprise but didn't let it register on her face. Adrian was going to give her the key to his apartment. This was a big deal to her. The man was willing to give her a key to his apartment but was still refusing her the key to his heart?

Chapter 18

Now that the Carnival season was over till next year, so, too, were all her outbursts of love. At all costs, Cory avoided any mention of love and relationships with Adrian. She still couldn't get over how incredibly dumb she had been. What was she thinking?

She knew she initially entered this fling just for the sex. What made her think that it would mean anything more for Adrian? Besides, what was better than exhilarating, no-strings-attached free sex for a man? Especially for a man like Adrian? Even when her feelings grew stronger by the day for him, she withheld from expressing them. Even when it was heart-wrenching and killing her emotionally inside, she still held them back.

Hence, she put off introducing Adrian to her father for as long as she could. What was she going to say? "Hi, Dad, meet Adrian, my sex buddy?" But Cory felt that her father should at least meet the man she was spending all this time with. She also knew her father well enough to know he'd soon begin asking too many questions. Adrian was the man she loved.

No. He was the man she loved sleeping with and sooner or later her father would just have to accept the fact. Cory planned to invite Adrian over to her house for dinner to meet her father and brother both.

"Do you want to take a walk?" Adrian asked her. They'd just finished having spicy tuna and shrimp tempura rolls at the Regent's sushi bar. Cory was crazy about the stuff but she had to coax and bribe Adrian to have it too.

"Sure, I'd love to."

Adrian held her hand as they exited through the back of the hotel. The sea behind them was calm as usual, the sky set aglow with magnificent hues of reds and deep oranges that signaled the setting sun for the evening. They took the stone pathway leading to the Waterfront. Walking hand in hand the two chatted away.

"And by the way, are you ever going to tell me why you really fled the States?" Cory asked.

"I didn't flee the States. What makes you think that happened?"

"Because something definitely has you all hung up. What's the deal with that?"

"Deal with what?"

Cory stopped walking and turned to face Adrian. "Look, it's obvious that something happened there for you to just pick yourself up and head back to Trinidad like that. And if my suspicions are correct, I'll say it was definitely because of a woman."

Cory apparently hit the nail right on the head. Adrian immediately stopped walking, too. "What?" There was a distant look in his eyes now. He didn't offer to say anything else.

"Adrian," Cory began rubbing her hand on his arm. "You can tell me. It's okay."

"Her name was Natacha," he began softly. "I fell for her and let's just say, I was left hanging."

"I'm sorry, Adrian."

"Nah. Don't be. That's water under the bridge now."

"Is it, though? It's obvious that you're still hurt over that, even though it has been what, a couple of years now."

"Cory, I was bitter mostly because all of this happened while I was far away fighting a war and Natacha turned to a good friend of mine for comfort. She couldn't handle me gone for so long. That's when they both realized that they were in love with each other." He shrugged. "When I came back home, she wasn't there to meet me. And that said it all for me. She opted out on me when I needed her the most."

"So why didn't she come to meet you?" Cory asked.

"She couldn't come. She was pregnant," Adrian answered.

"Oh my God," Cory gasped aloud. "*What?*"

"Yeah, but how could I really have expected her to go without sex for an entire year? C'mon she's a woman, she had needs."

"Yeah, but you had needs, too, Adrian," Cory blurted.

"Cory, when you're in a war zone, sex is probably the least of your worries. All you see is the light at the end of the tunnel. Completing your missions, finishing your tour, and coming home alive and in one piece."

"It's still terrible, Adrian." Cory wanted to wring this bitch's neck, who she never saw before in her life, for hurting her Adrian like that. How could she do that to him?

"Tell me about it. You know, I had made up my mind to marry her. I was going to ask her as soon as I got off that plane and I saw her. I tried my hardest to stay alive for her. Loving her was the only thing that kept me going so that we could have had a life together."

"Oh, Adrian." She of all people knew what that was like. "So are they still together?"

"Yep. Married with two kids the last I heard."

"At least we both have something in common. We were both left hanging by the people we loved just when we needed them the most," Cory said. She then told Adrian about Preston and how he couldn't handle her mourning the loss of her brother and mother. Preston had left her hanging, too. What a fool he turned out to be. Wasting three good years of her life and throwing away all they had together. All because he couldn't handle her grieving for her family.

Cory remembered Preston saying she was taking too long to get over it. That she didn't have time to give him what he really needed anymore. Imagine, what *he* needed? Well, what about her? She'd lost two family members in three months' time. What did he expect? Did one ever get over the death of a loved one, anyway?

That was when he turned to the loving arms of her skinny-bitch-of-a-cousin. Yes, her very own cousin. How much sadder could it have gotten than that? Then she dumped him after he refused to pay her rent and bills anymore. Guess who had the last laugh?

When they reached the huge water fountain feature, she and Adrian admired it in silence, immersed in their own thoughts.

"I'm also guessing Anna did the same thing, too. Coming back here to escape her divorce. So it seems like this island has become a place of refuge for the broken-hearted, don't you think?" Cory asked him.

"It would seem that way. But this is the best place to mend a broken heart."

"I'm really glad you told me this, Adrian." Cory turned to him. She only now realized what Adrian's entire hang-up had been from the start. He only used his job in the military as an excuse to not go down the relationship road again. He didn't have the time for a satisfying relationship because his job was holding him back? That seemed like such a load of bull-crap to her now. Now she knew the real reason. He was hurt very badly by this Natacha woman and wanted to make sure it never happened again with another. With her. Not that this revelation made her feel any better about her situation.

"This is lovely, don't you think?" Cory asked him, pointing at the huge water fountain, sprouting the water high into the air.

"Not as lovely as you are, Cory," Adrian kissed her on her forehead.

"You and that sweet talking," Cory laughed. "Hey, I have an idea. Why don't you come to my home for dinner? Meet my dad and brother."

"Sure, I'd love to. Are you finally going to cook for me, Cory?"

"Sure, as long as you can settle for a sandwich and a salad," Cory joked. "So how does 7:30 sound?"

"Good to me."

Chapter 19

Adrian showed up at Cory's house right on time, as usual. He had told her it was the military training; recruits were afforded little time to do almost everything: take a shower, eat a meal, even sleep, so one had no choice but to be punctual.

And which woman didn't like a punctual man? Not forgetting polite, mannerly, and helpful. One who was strong and could go the distance every time. Who would give his life for his country? And a girl could surely appreciate a man she could count on these days. She had to admit that the military did train their men well.

Cory had made it home just in time to shower, change, and set the table. She'd had to pick up the food she had ordered from the restaurant on her way home. The island offered a gastronomic feast for food lovers like herself, but Chinese was one of her favorite ethnic foods—next to authentic Indian, of course. She went overboard and ordered fried rice, stir-fried vegetables, lemon chicken, char sue pork, Cantonese shrimp, and Singapore noodles for dinner. That should be more than enough for the four of them. Then there was still that decadent triple-layered chocolate cake she got from Gabby for dessert.

"Hey, baby," Adrian greeted her with a warm one-armed hug as she opened the front door.

"These are for you." He presented her with a bunch of fresh lavender roses he had hiding behind his back.

"These are so beautiful. Thank you." The first thing she did was inhale their divine scent. "Now, how did you know I love lavender roses?"

"Let's just say, you smell just like them all the time."

"Wow, you *are* good."

"So what did you cook for me?"

"Um, Chinese," Cory giggled.

"I didn't know what we were having so I didn't know what kind of wine to buy. So will this do?" Adrian handed her the bottle, looking all optimistic.

"Pinot Noir," Cory read the label out loud. "Oh, yeah, this would do just fine. And even if it doesn't pair well, I'll ensure it doesn't go to waste. For a guy who doesn't really drink, you sure know your alcohol."

"Hey, I do learn from the best," he grinned. "And I mean that totally in a good way."

The evening started off well for everyone. When Cory introduced Adrian to her father, her father was civil toward him. It wasn't the warmest but at least it was civil. Adrian got along much better with Christian, who seemed totally fascinated by him. Their attempt at male bonding made Cory smile. Now, if only her father would just try the same, for her sake anyway.

They ate their meal pretty much in silence. It was nothing like having dinner with Anna the other night, Cory thought. Fascinating conversation and loud laughter had filled Adrian's apartment. A welcome addition to the usual loud moaning and groaning from their lovemaking. Neither was it like meeting the entire Mendez clan at the anniversary party, but Cory still tried her best to steer the little conversation they managed in the right direction.

As the night wore on, Cory noticed the expression on her father's humorless face growing colder. Something had him unhappy. It couldn't be Adrian, because he had been the perfect gentleman all evening long. It wasn't until her father sprung the question that was possibly eating at him all along that things took a drastic nose dive for the worse.

"So, Adrian, what do you do for a living?" Jonathan Phillips finally asked.

"Dad?" Cory immediately interjected. "What does Adrian's job have to do with anything?"

"It's okay, Cory," Adrian spoke up. "I'm a second lieutenant in the army, sir. Currently I'm attached to a task force in Port of

Spain that handles extremely violent criminal behavior."

There was definitely tension in the air now.

"So you're a soldier?"

"Yes, I am, sir," Adrian replied.

"Adrian used to be a U.S. Marine, Dad. He even fought in Afghanistan," Cory added.

"So you fought under Bush?"

"Yes, I did, sir."

"That's the thing. Who gave you all the right to barge into somebody else's country and just take over like that?"

A few seconds of silence passed before Cory squealed, "Dad? What're you doing?" knocking over her glass of wine in the process. Christian began feverishly wiping up the spill.

"With all due respect, sir, I was there. I saw firsthand what was going on. These people weren't free. They were under siege from the Taliban. Men, women, and children were being mercilessly killed over there." Adrian's eyes never left Cory's father.

"Spoken like a true American. I see you still have your American sentiments intact and I'm not surprised," Jonathan replied coldly.

"This has nothing to do with my American sentiments, sir, because I also have my Trinidadian sentiments as equally intact," Adrian answered. His voice was beginning to rise from anxiety, "This is a war effort to rid the world of terrorist threats so that people can go about their daily lives in peace."

"Adrian, don't even waste your time trying to explain anything," Cory interjected, disgusted and embarrassed beyond belief.

Adrian wasn't finished yet. "Don't forget that Trinidadian citizens also lost their lives in the World Trade Center. I cherished the opportunity to serve as a U.S. Marine under a United States of America-led war in Afghanistan. And if ever it's required of me to serve my country in that capacity again, I'll be more than honored to do it. Sir," Adrian ended forcefully, ensuring Mr. Phillips got his point.

Everyone at the table again went completely silent. Cory looked back and forth at her father's cold, now angry expression, then back at Adrian again. The silence was finally broken when Jonathan stood up from his seat, the chair scraping back against the tiled floor.

"Well, what can I say to that," Jonathan began. "You were obviously there, young man, and I obviously wasn't. So I stand corrected. Now, if you all will excuse me." Jonathan then removed himself quietly from the room. As his short and stocky frame retreated, he left everyone a little more than stunned at the table.

"Adrian, I'm so sorry about this," Cory began.

"Cory, it's okay. I'm accustomed to this kind of stuff. I hear it all the time," Adrian said. "Baby, please stop crying," he pleaded with her as the tears started.

Christian was next to excuse himself from the table without saying anything other than good night to both of them.

"Adrian, I need to explain something to you. I should've told you this before. My dad doesn't like the police . . . or soldiers . . . well, the entire military on the whole. Remember, I told you that I lost my brother?"

"Yes," Adrian answered.

"Well, I never told you how," Cory exhaled a deep breath. "My brother was killed by the police."

"What?" Then he exploded. "Cory, why after all this time did you never once tell me about this?"

"I don't know, Adrian. I just wanted so much to forget the entire thing ever happened."

"So what did he do wrong, Cory?"

"That's the thing. Nothing. Collin never did anything wrong. He was completely innocent. He never did anything wrong," she sobbed even more now. "The police murdered my brother, Adrian."

Adrian went completely silent. He remained silent until Cory told him the entire story of what few details she knew surrounding the death of her brother.

"So . . . this is the reason why you hated the police, Cory?" Adrian finally asked her.

"Yes." It wasn't her family alone either that this happened to. Many others like hers had to deal with innocent members being killed by the police. And with no avenue for recourse. Civilian casualties didn't only occur in the Middle East.

"And this is the reason why your father hates the entire military?"

"Yes."

Adrian shook his head. "Cory, you should have told me this before I came here to your house. Now, not only do I feel like I've disrespected your father in his own house. I feel like a complete idiot."

Cory was afraid to even look Adrian in the eyes now. For the first time since she knew him, he was sounding very angry. He was angry at her. This was the first time she even heard him speak at the top of his voice like that. And it was all her fault.

"When you told me that your brother was killed, Cory, I thought he was killed in an accident or something. Not by the police," Adrian said. "And I never prodded you because you never wanted to talk about it."

"Adrian, I'm really, really sorry about this."

"*Sorry?* I mean, your brother was killed by the police, Cory, and you neglected to tell me something like that?" Adrian ignored her apologies. "Have you forgotten that I *work* with the police every day? Look at me, Cory," he demanded.

But she turned around and picked up a framed photograph on the buffet behind her instead. It was one of her and Collin together, smiling. The photo was taken just one month before he was killed, for his birthday.

"I never introduced you. Adrian, this is my brother, Collin." Cory showed the photo to Adrian. He glanced at it, clearly in no mood to be looking at any photos. "We were inseparable growing up," Cory was saying. "We're only a year apart, just like you and Anna."

*

Adrian wasn't really listening to her, he was concentrating so intensely on that photo now. Cory and the young man were hugging and smiling. He looked just like her. He too had wild, curly hair, only his was much shorter. There was something about him that Adrian couldn't quite pin down. He felt like he'd met him somewhere before. Then something clicked. His memory flashed. He started to feel numb, his body went cold. All he remembered feeling was the warm blood quickly draining away from his body. He panicked. Then he bolted.

Chapter 20

Driving home from Cory's house, Adrian's mood was solemn. His head was clouded with ominous thoughts. The entire evening kept replaying over and over in his mind.

The police murdered my brother, Adrian.

He heard Cory's voice over and over in his head saying that.

Adrian, this is my brother, Collin.

No, it just couldn't be possible. Could life once again be this cruel to him?

Adrian couldn't reach his apartment quickly enough. By the time he did, he was sick to the stomach, cold sweating and all. He rushed into his bathroom and splashed some cold water on his face. That felt better but when he looked at his reflection in the mirror, it was ghostly pale.

*

The sound of the alarm woke him at 5:00 a.m. Adrian's eyes immediately flew open. He had to go to work today. He realized that he had fallen asleep in his dress clothes and that he was crossways on the bed. He must have been more tired than he expected. He had to practically drag himself out of bed. He remembered bits of last night but hoped it was all a bad dream. When he felt the ferocious pangs of a headache coming on, it told him otherwise.

In the kitchen, he turned on the water for his morning coffee. Adrian changed out of his clothes and stepped into the shower. The blasting cold water this morning was exactly what he needed. He felt like crap. Hell, if he didn't know any better, he would have said he had a hangover. He had one scotch on the rocks last night with Cory's father earlier on in the evening and only because he didn't want to insult the man. But this he eventually managed in the end. Just when everything was going so good for him.

He could have done with some more sleep but Adrian knew he had a full day ahead. It was only two days before the start of a summit he and his men were expected to provide protection for, so his hands were full. In fact, all military personnel on the island would be busy. His lack of sleep, this annoying headache, and Lord knows what else he'd have to contend with today made him extremely grumpy.

He headed for the gym, his second usual morning custom. As Adrian was driving out, the sun was rising over the magnificent hills. It was truly a breathtaking sight to behold but not even that could cheer him from his mood. Neither did the coffee, cold shower, or his routine workout.

By the time he did get to work and changed into uniform, the hectic pace immediately set in for the day. Maybe this was a good thing. Maybe it would take his mind off his personal problems for a while. Maybe he would be able to forget about last night at Cory's house. Her dead brother, her father, her . . . everything.

His team was part of a big military exercise in the hills again. This time, with a much larger contingent comprising well over two hundred officers from other divisions, soldiers, and tracker dogs. This was no ordinary exercise. This type usually went from house-to-house thoroughly searching for arms and ammunitions, drugs and specific criminal elements that were wanted in connection with several criminal investigations. When they were briefed, it was time to lock and load.

"Let's roll," Adrian signaled his team. Vehicle loads of them moved out and converged on the outskirts of the capital and very soon the exercise was underway. Officers were moving from house to house conducting the search and the occupants were not happy. They voiced their visible displeasure every chance they got. The constant whirring of chopper blades hovering low signaled the military's strong intent of an all out war on crime today.

Everything seemed to be going as planned until a murder

suspect was found hiding out in a dilapidated shack. That was when the chaos erupted. When the handcuffed suspect was being taken away into custody, a mob of angry villagers proclaiming his innocence began attacking officers and soldiers.

Stones and bottles began raining down on them as the mob grew larger and angrier by the minute. The roads were blockaded with debris, then set on fire. One police vehicle's windscreen was smashed and the glass shattered everywhere.

"Not today, man," Adrian groaned under his breath. The entire atmosphere quickly erupted into a mini-riot and this was one angry crowd, shouting and hurling obscenities at them. Officers were retaliating in return, fending off their attackers the best way they could. Members of the media were quick on the scene filming footage for their breaking news stories. It was ugly.

In the middle of this, Adrian felt his cell phone vibrating. "Not now." When he checked, it was Cory calling. He definitely couldn't talk to her now. The phone vibrated again after he ignored it the first time. It was Cory again.

Adrian was having a hard enough time concentrating on this task at hand, he honestly couldn't deal with Cory. He would have to explain to her what happened when that time came. By the looks of things, he'd have many things to explain to Cory. Adrian switched off his cell just as a flying missile came aiming for his head.

Chapter 21

It was a successful exercise despite the mini-riot that broke out on the hills. The situation had calmed down considerably and things came under control when other arrests were made, close to one hundred for various offenses. By the time Adrian's unit got back to base several hours later, the police had a huge haul of illegal guns to process. Not forgetting ammunition rounds, cocaine, and marijuana.

When he switched on his cell again in the relative calm of his office, he noticed five missed calls from Cory. There were also e-mails, texts, and other messages. Adrian didn't return any of them. He didn't know what he was going to say to her just yet. He couldn't even explain why he'd bolted from her house last night. He couldn't focus clearly on anything until he knew for sure.

It was another long day for Adrian and the remainder of the week went in pretty much the same manner. Since it was pre-summit week, their security arrangements were pushed into high gear now. All the months of training for this were finally bearing fruit. They were busy with patrols and random security checks in the city. They manned roadblocks and provided added security details for entire delegations arriving.

Adrian's work hours went into overdrive. Twenty-four-hour shifts turned into forty-eight-hours and more for him. He literally only had time to sleep for a few hours, eat, and shower in-between. By the time he realized it, he hadn't spoken to Cory for a couple of days. Adrian knew how worried and better yet, how pissed off, she would be by now but he wasn't prepared to deal with her just yet. He had to do something first.

The phone rang and rang before Anna finally answered it. "Hey, bro," she said.

"I suppose you're so busy that you can't even call your own brother," Adrian returned.

"I'm so swamped, Adrian, you won't believe. I'm in overdrive for this summit. Can't wait for it to end!"

"I know what you mean, sis. Don't worry, it's exactly the same with me on this end."

"So what's going on?"

"I need a huge favor, Anna. And you're the best bet I have right now. I need some information but I don't have time to get it myself."

"So what do you need?" Anna asked him.

"I need you to search for a news story for me. I'm sure you all carried it. It was a police shooting about two years ago. Four men were shot."

"Do you have an exact date or the names of these men?"

"I can't remember the date exactly but it was in early March. Check for a Collin Phillips," Adrian ended.

"Collin Phillips? Is he related to Cory?" Anna immediately asked.

Adrian went silent. He figured he had to be straight with her. She was actually helping him out here.

"That's her brother."

"Cory's brother was shot by the police!" Anna exclaimed. "Why?"

Adrian really had to cut Anna short for the moment because he wasn't too sure himself. "So how soon can you get this for me, Anna?" he asked.

"I'm going back on air in a few minutes but I'll work on it as soon as I get a spare moment. How soon do you need it?"

"Like yesterday," Adrian quickly responded. "Send it to my cell, okay."

"Okay, sure. I gotta go, Adrian," and Anna hastily ended the call with him.

Now all he had to do was wait on her e-mail to be positively sure about this one. His future with Cory depended on it.

*

It was summit weekend and the military-police units were making their presence felt in all the gang-riddled areas in and around the city, keeping a watchful eye out for any unwanted trouble. Adrian was a bit on edge. He didn't know which was worse. Waiting on Anna or waiting on Anna in Gangsta-ville.

But these hills were such a beautiful place, offering one of the most breathtaking views on the island. Adrian looked down, concentrating on the developing modern city mixed in with the historic remnants of the city's colonial past below him. But the criminal elements gave the area such a notorious reputation and made things bad for everyone here.

Everyone knew wherever there were illegal drugs passing through, there were bound to be the guns which ultimately fuelled the gang warfare and spurred on the criminal behavior. And the Caribbean was a known transshipment point for the producers of the south to get to their large markets in the north. And that was just the way things worked around here.

His sister finally came through for him. When his phone buzzed and beeped, Adrian immediately downloaded the clip Anna sent. Her voice could be heard reading the evening news: "Four men were reportedly shot and killed by police in Port of Spain last night. One of them, according to his relatives, is innocent. Collin Phillips was on his way home when he was apparently car-jacked by three known members of a gang. A shootout then ensued with task-force police and soldiers killing all four men at the scene."

That was all Adrian needed to hear. A photo of Collin Phillips came on his screen. "No!" Adrian shouted at the phone.

The word "innocent" reverberated through Adrian's head. So this was the reason why Cory and her entire family hated the police so much and by extension the entire military. They had killed her brother. He should have remembered that face. He should have remembered that name but there had to be thousands of people on this island with that same last name.

It finally dawned on Adrian. He had to accept this fact. It wasn't *they* who killed Cory's brother. No matter how hard Adrian had tried to forget that night ever happened, the grim, harsh reality all rushed back to him. *He* killed Collin Phillips. *He* had killed Cory's brother. He'd killed the brother of the woman he loved. How was he ever going to explain this to Cory?

Two years ago and fresh to this task force, he had gone out on a routine patrol with police officers and his soldiers. There were eight of them in the vehicle that night. He remembered them receiving an all-points-bulletin for a vehicle with three suspects. They had just robbed and killed an off-duty police officer in the city. Everyone knew the officer who died. He was one of them.

It all happened so quickly. The suspects were last seen heading right toward them, on the outskirts of the capital. They were ready and on the lookout. When they saw the vehicle approaching, the occupants were firstly warned to stop. Then they began receiving hostile fire from the men in the vehicle. They had no other choice but to open fire in return. And all eight of them had. The car soon crashed into a nearby wall at the side of the road. When silence fell and it was quiet again, there were four motionless bodies in that car.

Four bodies? The APB had said to be on the lookout for three suspects. Who was the fourth man? Where did he come from? They had all wondered about that. As it turned out, the extra body was that of the driver of the vehicle who had received the most gunshot wounds. He had to be taken out first so that the vehicle would come to a stop.

Adrian remembered there was a strange look on the driver's face. He only realized afterward what that look was. It was the look of confusion. Adrian was the one who felt for a pulse, checking to see if he was still alive. His blood was hot, gushing out of his fresh wounds. Blood was oozing from his wild, curly hair. Adrian had desperately wanted him to live. The driver wasn't even armed. Adrian didn't want to have an innocent man's blood on his hands.

Adrian had questioned himself over and over. Should they have used such lethal force on these men? He prayed that the fourth man was not innocent as initially reported. However, there was strong evidence produced which suggested that he was. He had not one prior criminal record. He wasn't known to the police. He was just a normal young man on his way home from work that evening when he was carjacked by a group of bandits and murderers.

The eight of them at the scene that night were interviewed by their superiors and submitted individual reports on everything dealing with the shootings. Based on this, a formal investigation was never launched into the matter and their names were never revealed to the public.

The ballistic tests on the weapons used by the three suspects confirmed that they were involved in the shooting death of a police officer and several other people before that. When the investigations were carried out after, it was confirmed that the driver of the vehicle had been an innocent victim. The death of Collin Phillips was ruled as an accidental police shooting. He was in the wrong place at the wrong time.

Adrian tried to forget that incident for two years. Now, it was back to haunt him in the worst way possible. Only this time, it could cost him the woman he loved. The woman he would give his own life to protect.

*

When the summit finally ended on Sunday and Adrian got off on Monday morning, he was physically and emotionally beat. All he could think of was Cory. He just couldn't afford to lose her now over all this.

Adrian knew Cory deserved the truth. Honesty was at the top of her requirement list, for God's sake. Yet, how could he find it in his heart to tell her something so devastating?

He hadn't spoken to Cory for days now. It felt more like a year. He missed her terribly. Her giggles, her smile, her teasing him to insanity when they made love. He was going crazy from not seeing her.

Adrian mentally went over his options as he paced the kitchen floor. The poor tiles were probably worn from his frantic back-and-forth pacing. He could tell Cory, explain everything to her and run the risk of losing her. This way, he would at least come clean. But what if he couldn't bring himself to tell her, she probably would never find out. What she didn't know would never hurt her, right?

But what if by some small chance she did find out? What then? A voice in Adrian's head kept asking. But how could she find out? Another was asking.

The only family member who knew about this was his aunt and only because she was a high-ranking officer. He never even told Anna because she worked for a state-owned media house. If any of her colleagues had gotten hold of that information, it surely would have been damaging to her career. And he surely wasn't going to let that happen to his only sister. Not after all she had been through with her divorce. He also had his two nephews to think about.

He was raised to do the right thing. He considered himself a man of honor and courage. He knew all this but was he prepared to face the consequences after? Adrian was so afraid about this one. Afraid that yet another woman would walk out of his life when he needed her the most.

After much pondering and soul searching, Adrian finally made up his mind about it. There was nothing else left for him to do if he wanted Cory in his life, and he absolutely did.

It was a little before five in the afternoon when he pulled up to her office building.

His hands shook from nerves. *It's your only option, Adrian.* No turning back now, he kept reminding himself. He was early. He parked in front the five-story building and waited for her. She had to walk this way to get to her car. Adrian's only company was the ever so often gentle hum of the engine as the air-conditioning cooled the interior. This faint rise and fall irritated the hell out of him.

Half an hour ticked by ever so slowly and Adrian was losing all his resolve by the minute. Just as he was about to dial her number, he saw her walking out with Jay. They were talking intensely about something. He didn't know why he felt an instant jolt of jealousy threatening.

Cory hadn't noticed him there but when Adrian called out to her, she totally ignored him and deliberately looked straight through him. She kept on walking.

To stop her, Adrian quickly reached for her arm. That was when he was thankful that Jay excused himself.

"Baby, please." Then he reached for her cheek and softly caressed it. He could only see pain in her eyes.

"Please don't touch me, Adrian."

Adrian immediately dropped his hand to his side and said, "Cory, I'm sorry I didn't return your calls. I know you must be really angry with me right now. But I was so caught up with work these past days with the summit."

"Yeah, I know. But a simple returned phone call when you got a spare moment would've done the trick, I think," she angrily lashed back at him.

"Cory, again, I'm truly sorry," he quietly said.

"So that's it? I haven't seen or heard from you for days and that's all you can come up it. Please, Adrian, I'm not a fool, okay."

"Cory, I haven't even gotten enough sleep during the last how many days. We were working round the clock."

"So that's the reason you're looking like this?" Cory asked. "And you're hurt."

"Not really," Adrian quickly responded. "Just a small accident I had."

"The last time I saw you, Adrian, you just left me there feeling so completely humiliated and like such a fool. You were so angry with me."

"Cory, yes I was angry at first but . . . look, I know you must've been worried and I owe you a huge apology." *So that's what she thought this was all about? She thought that he was angry with her?* "I really am very sorry, baby."

"I thought you had abandoned me, Adrian," she added softly.

"Cory, never! Why would I ever want to abandon you?" Adrian took her into his arms and held her. She felt so stiff there. He knew how hard it had been for him, he could only imagine what it must have been like for her. "I have all that I could possibly ever need with you, Cory. That's why I need to talk to you about something."

"Now?" she asked in an agitated tone.

"Yes, now. Do you have somewhere else to go?" This couldn't wait any longer.

"Not really. So what is it, then?"

"Let's go. I want to take you somewhere."

"So where're we going?" she enquired, when he passed his apartment.

"Do you trust me?" Adrian asked in return.

"Yes," Cory answered. "Unfortunately."

Adrian drove in silence. They went up and around a hilly roadway. Round and round and up and up they went. When Adrian finally pulled into a compound, the sign said, Welcome to Fort George Historical Site.

Adrian held her hand as he helped her out. There was an eerie quiet to the place. Only a handful of people milled about the Fort, mainly tourists taking pictures.

"It's so beautiful and so peaceful up here," was all she could manage. "I'm positive you can see the entire island from up here."

Adrian agreed with her as he moved to hold her around the waist. His hands immediately snaked around her, gently pulling her closer to him. He underestimated the power of this and what holding Cory so close could do to him.

"Cory, believe me when I say just how much I really missed you."

"If you really missed me that much Adrian, why didn't you return any of my calls?" Cory demanded. "Or texts. Or e-mails?"

She wiggled out of his grasp then and started walking toward the many cannons that lined the Fort. She climbed atop one and perched herself comfortably on the cannon. "I absolutely love it here," she whispered.

Cory was such a vision to behold. Sitting on that cannon, her hair blowing freely in the breeze. Adrian couldn't wait anymore, "Cory, I should've told you this all along. But I was just trying to deny it so many times. And I can't anymore. You mean more to me than anything in this world and I'm really thankful that you're in my life right now," he finally let out. "The things I went through this last week, Cory, they only made me realize that I really can't be without you in my life. I love you too much . . . I'm in love with you, Cory."

Adrian paused briefly for a deep breath. He was reaching very deep to get this out right. He covered her small hands with one of his and reached into his pockets for something with his other hand. A small, dark blue box came out.

Then Adrian got down on bended knees. "Cory, I'll be honored if you'd be my wife. Will you marry me?"

Chapter 22

What? Cory nearly fell off the cannon in shock. She was nowhere near to expecting Adrian to just spring this question on her like that. The big question. The question every woman dreams of being asked at one point or the other in her life. She was at a total loss for words.

She had to steady herself on the cannon.

"Adrian, what're you asking me?" was all she could muster at this point. Then he opened the box in his hand. And there it lay. Sparkling in the setting sun. The ring. No, the most beautiful solitaire she'd ever seen stared back at her. How did he know? This was her dream ring. Ever since she was a little girl, Cory had dreamed and imagined what this day would be like. Nothing she had come up with then could have compared to this moment now.

Adrian was looking at her expectantly, probably waiting on her answer. Tears welled in her eyes.

"Do you really love me, Adrian? Because if you're playing with me . . . ."

"I'm not playing, Cory," Adrian interrupted her. "I've fallen so completely in love with you. I adore you. I came to this island never expecting anything really. And here I was able to find you. To find love. Baby, I've never needed anyone like I do you, Cory. If that answers your question?"

Cory had wanted to hear these words coming from Adrian so much. The tears started slowly rolling down her cheeks now. "Yeah, but are you seriously asking me to marry you?"

"Yes, I am, Cory. I've never been more serious in my life. If I didn't want you to be my wife, I wouldn't have asked you such a question. I want this more than anything," he smiled. That gorgeous, heartwarming smile that made her feel like flying with angels.

"Then, yes. I'll marry you, baby." Adrian quickly slipped the solitaire onto her wedding finger. "I'll be everything you need."

Cory smiled between the tears as Adrian lifted her off the cannon. "I love you so much, Adrian. I can't even describe what I'm feeling right now. I'm just so happy, baby," she said.

Overcome with emotion, Cory was laughing and crying at the same time. She quickly forgot the anger she had felt earlier. She was now experiencing the greatest feeling in the world. It was indescribable, the moment unforgettable. She was literally on top of the world, high up on the most beautiful fort, more than a thousand feet above the city. In one of the most breathtaking and most romantic places on the island and the man she loved more than anything just unexpectedly proposed to her. Cory couldn't help but wonder if Adrian's reason for proposing here had anything to do with the fort's military history. That would definitely be a very sentimental thing for him. Fort George was a military fortification built in 1804 by the British to protect the capital from invaders.

Adrian had been in love with her all the while. He wanted her to be his wife. So nothing else mattered. Cory was so close to being in heaven right now. She kissed him. She never wanted to let go of him. She thought she might wake up at any moment and this would all be a dream if she ever let go of him. It felt so surreal. Only this was so real.

"I love you so much," Adrian said again.

When Cory suggested that they get married sooner rather than later, Adrian was only too happy to oblige. First, she had the daunting task of telling her father about their impending nuptials. So far, she only wore her engagement ring when she was with Adrian because of the disaster that nearly erupted when both men met. Cory knew she had to prepare herself for another battle.

When she finally mustered the courage, she came home from work early one afternoon. Albeit, she was a nervous wreck, Cory really felt that a heart-to-heart talk with her father was the best way to tell him the good news. Her father never tried to actually hide how he really felt about Adrian, so this was going to be very difficult indeed. She knew she was going to do her best sales pitch as clearly and as quickly as possible. She had to sell her love for Adrian and his love for her and the fact that they wanted to be together.

They were doing the right thing by getting married, anyway. Her father should be happy about that. They weren't going to just move in and live together as was the norm these days. Cory knew he would hit the roof and probably disown her in the process if she ever decided to do that. She also hoped that maturity would prevail and he would try to be happy for his only daughter.

"Hey, Dad," Cory cheerfully greeted her father as she planted a big kiss on his cheek, something she hadn't done in a while.

"Hi, Princess. You're home early today."

"Yeah, I know. Isn't that great though? I can finally spend some quality time with my favorite dad." She passed her hand through his straight graying hair.

"Okay, what do you want?" an ever-alert Jonathan asked.

Cory threw her handbag and car keys on the coffee table and grabbed an armchair next to him in the living room.

"What makes you think I want anything?" she asked, with a broad smile spreading on her face.

"So what's all of this about, then? The cheerfulness, the kiss, the . . . ."

"Dad, I always kiss you," Cory said.

"Not anymore, you don't," he huffed.

"Oh, forget it. I do have some good news, though," she announced.

"Please tell me that you got a big promotion so I can finally retire."

"Dad? You're retiring next year, anyway."

"Okay, okay. So what's your good news?"

Cory took a deep breath. "Adrian asked me to marry him, Dad."

She waited for her father's response. Silence. After what seemed like an eternity, Cory asked, "Dad, did you hear what I just said?"

"I heard," Jonathan replied coldly as he removed his glasses. "So what's the rush? Are you pregnant, Cory?"

"Dad . . . no!" a horrified Cory exclaimed. "We just love each other and we want to get married."

"This is all happening rather quickly, don't you think? I mean you only just introduced the guy to me two weeks ago."

"Yes, I know that . . . but we've been seeing each other before that. We know what we're getting into, Dad."

"Do you? Well, something just isn't sitting well with me on this one, Cory," he said, playing with his well-trimmed graying beard.

"Dad, I just want you to be happy for me. Besides, you have always wanted to walk me down the aisle and give me away on my wedding day, right?"

"I don't think I'm prepared to do that under these circumstances."

"What circumstances? Dad . . . what're you saying?" a shaky Cory asked.

"Cory, you're an intelligent girl. I just cannot accept this whole marriage proposal thing . . . something just doesn't seem right. So I'm telling you from now. Don't expect me to be at this wedding," Jonathan said matter-of-factly.

Cory couldn't believe what she was hearing. Was her father refusing to even attend his only daughter's wedding?

"I think you should really listen to me and not go against my wishes. Take your time, Cory . . . get to know this young man some more before you rush off and make the biggest mistake of your life," Jonathan pleaded with her.

"Dad, you're being so unfair to Adrian. You don't even know him. He really is a good, decent man. He's not like the others.

I told you he's different. Why are you being so stereotypical?" There, she finally said it to her father's face.

Those words felt strange coming from her own mouth. A few months ago she had been the very same way but at least she was smart enough to have overcome it. She owed this all to Adrian. He was successful in making her see things differently. This was the first lesson he had taught her on only the first day.

"Well, Cory, I guess I don't want to see my only daughter get hurt and then divorced and then end up as another single mother living on this island."

"Dad, that's not going to happen. You and Mom were married soon after meeting each other too," she shot back.

"That was different. This is not one of those damn romance novels you read all the time. This is real life."

"I know this is real life. This is *my* life," she shouted. Cory inhaled deeply, trying to calm herself. "Look, Dad. I'm really tired . . . I'm so tired of having to fight you about everything ever since Mom died. And you know what? I am going to marry Adrian whether you like it or not. And if you don't want to be at our wedding, well, then that's your choice. No one's forcing you but do know that this wedding is going to happen, with or without your blessings."

With that, she purposely walked away and left a shocked Jonathan still sitting there. When she opened the door to her bedroom, the tears started rushing down her cheeks. Her entire body shook with violent sobs. *What did you really expect, Cory? You were a fool to think he'd ever accept Adrian.*

She pulled out the stack of boxes from beneath her bed and began to grab clothing out of her closet and angrily shoved them into the boxes.

Cory finally felt the need to be set free and be on her own again. And this was the best opportunity she had so she was going to take it. Cory slipped her engagement ring onto her finger, for good this time. Between her tears, she was admiring the fine quality of the sparkling diamond in the light, thinking about the wedding and what her new life with Adrian would be like. There was a bitter-sweet feeling in her heart but finally, she was going to marry her knight.

Chapter 23

It was actually Adrian's idea for them to get married on the beautiful sister isle of Tobago. He had told Cory about joking with his mother at JFK, the day he returned to Trinidad. To make her feel better, he had promised her an invitation to a tropical wedding in paradise one day. His mother always loved the idea of a wedding on a Caribbean beach. It never even crossed his mind then that it would actually be *his* wedding.

Cory thought it was a fantastic idea. Tobago was one of the most fought-over islands throughout the entire Caribbean and she couldn't blame them. The island was just spectacular. The beautiful calm beaches, the Buccoo Reef, the waterfalls, the magnificent sunsets. It was nothing like her sister Trinidad, always busy with the hustle and bustle of everyday life. Tobago was always serene and so romantic. Thus, it was the perfect choice for their wedding and honeymoon.

Within a few weeks, all the hectic preparations were in place for their wedding day. Due to the time factor, it was pretty much a very intimate gathering on the beach. Cory didn't want to spend another day apart from Adrian, especially with the way her father had been acting.

Everything about this wedding was going to be simple and beautiful. Cory chose a dress made by a local designer for her big day. It wasn't white in its entirety as there were beautiful hand-painted tropical flowers down the front of it. She had spotted it in a local magazine and just fell completely in love with it. For Cory, it was perfect for a beach-themed wedding and it suited her style. Form-fitting and elegant with a sexy low cut back. Just like the dress she was wearing when she and Adrian saw each other the first time at the police station.

She wore a pair of flat white sandals encrusted with crystals. Cory left her hair out, curly and wild, blowing in the wind. Her ensemble was completed with a small bouquet of tropical flowers made with pink and green hybrid anthoriums, matching the flowers on her dress.

As Cory walked down the white sandy beach to where Adrian was waiting for her, the melodious sounds of the island's steel pan drifted in the breeze. Stevie Wonder's "Ribbon in the Sky" was being expertly played. A little too retro for her but so beautiful all the same.

She was determined to completely immerse herself into this beautiful moment, despite the fact that most of her family was not able to celebrate with her. Her father had downright refused to be here but her mother and brother were definitely present in spirit. She could feel them around her as she walked. Two angels on either side of her, their white wings fluttering in the gentle sea breezes blowing through her hair. Only Christian and her grandmother who lived in Tobago attended.

The wedding was being held one Friday afternoon in late April, on the private beach of a villa they rented in Bacolet. As she walked, the most picturesque backdrop of the sun over a beautiful expanse of calm, sparkling turquoise waters filled her eyes. The sounds of seagulls crying as they dove into the water for their meal intermixed with the steel pan and the evening tide crashing into the salty rocks on the cliff filled her ears. The sight of Adrian standing there, waiting for her, his white shirt fluttering, filled her heart. It could not have been more perfect.

*

As she neared him, Adrian felt his breath slowly being taken away, just like the gentle breeze blowing her curls about her face. He had never seen Cory look more beautiful and in just a few minutes, she was going to be his wife. He was going to love and cherish her forever. As time went by, he heard less and less of those voices in his head, arguing that he must tell her about her brother. Hopefully, they were gone forever.

When Cory finally reached her destination, Adrian took her hands in his and they exchanged their precious marriage vows to each other in the presence of his mother Dianne, who flew in from New York to celebrate with them; Anna-Marie and his nephews; Christian; Cory's grandmother; Adrian's best man and cousin, Rafael; Elisha, her maid of honor; Curtis, Elisha's husband; and of course, Jay.

Unfortunately, Gabby was in the U.S. preparing for the birth of her first niece or nephew and Kerry couldn't get the time off from work. Or so she had said.

It was a short but sweet ceremony with little extravagance. Yet, it was the perfect wedding to Cory. She had dreamed about her wedding day since she was a little girl but her actual wedding day was nothing like her dreams. There were no white limousine, no huge bridal party, no long white train and crystal encrusted wedding dress or hundreds of people she barely knew. But this was so much better. She didn't need all those things anymore. Nothing mattered anymore, as long as Adrian was her husband.

The warm Caribbean nights became even steamier in the honeymoon suite. As her nails dug into the hard contoured muscles of Adrian's back, the tears rolled down her cheeks. The sheer intensity of pleasure she experienced from his amazing love, only left her craving more. Cory could never get over Adrian's mad desire; he never seemed to get enough of her. No matter how many times they had made love, it always felt like the first time they were discovering each other. Today, the two of them became one. She had all she could ever need. She was finally complete.

Chapter 24

His precious forty inch plasma and Wii games were the first to go. To move out of the bedroom that was. But with the stuff Cory was serving up in there, who needed ESPN or *Call of Duty*?

He was also out of closet space and had to endure *Lifetime* movie marathons on the weekends or *Food Network* reruns. Since it was his first time actually living with a woman, Adrian figured they all came with being married.

Life was good for him. The nagging voices in his head had stopped. Cory was happy, so he was happy. Though, not for the life of him would he ever comprehend why she really needed thirty-two pairs of shoes!

He enjoyed the simple things like watching her apply her lip gloss in the mirror. The way she pouted those sexy lips of hers and the seductive way she would bend her body, sticking out her gorgeous butt he loved like that. Cory didn't even realize just how incredibly sexy she looked doing that and how instantly he was turned on by just looking at her do it. That was a sight Adrian knew he wouldn't tire of anytime soon.

*

Cory could finally exhale. Life was perfect for the first time in a long time for her. After spending two glorious weeks in laid-back Tobago, touring and exploring, making love for hours and laughing all afternoon long on the beaches, it was back to the fast pace and grind. Back to work, back to the office, and adjusting to married life. Adrian ensured she was comfortable and settled in quickly, even if it meant putting himself out of his way at times. Okay, maybe all the time.

Her life had changed so drastically these past few months. Who would have thought that getting her car stolen would have landed her a husband? Cory never expected that a sweet, wonderful man would have come into her life anytime. She always referred to herself as "glutton for punishment" but for once, she wasn't being punished.

Since she always came home to him, after an extremely hard day at work Adrian always helped her to relax and unwind. A long, warm soak in the tub, her favorite glass of wine, followed by one of his sensuous body massages which often led to lazy, erotic evenings in the bedroom.

Cory fell more and more in love with him with each passing day, week, and month. It was amazing just how attentive to her needs he really was. She usually rewarded him with sexy lingerie or an erotic strip tease, tempting and teasing his mind and body senseless. It felt great falling asleep in Adrian's arms at nights and waking up with him still there on mornings.

On the down side, there were the military exercises and the high degree of danger involved all the time. Cory knew Adrian spared her the gory daily details of his job. Though she went absolutely crazy not being able to see him for twenty-four hours at a time, she made up for this by jogging with Elisha and Gabby around the Savannah. But when she and Adrian did see each other, it was pure loving all over again.

Like what she had in store for him tonight. Cory was feeling naughty all afternoon at work. Maybe it was because of the racy text message Adrian had sent her, getting her hormones raging and pumping hot. On her way home, she stopped at her favorite store in the mall for some new lingerie and couldn't wait to get home to her man. After dinner and a long Gardenia-infused bubble bath, Cory was just about ready to jump his bones.

She posed provocatively against the doorway in her sexy black number, wearing her favorite floral scent, the one that smelled like lavender roses she knew he loved. With his keen senses, he would definitely know when she entered the room. Adrian was busy working on something on his laptop and like clockwork, without having to say a word, he turned in his swivel chair.

"Whoa! You look hot, baby," Adrian appreciatively exclaimed.

Cory slowly and sensually sauntered over to him. She seductively bent her body to meet his height level on the chair, making sure he got a generous view of her ample cleavage in the process. Her breasts looked bigger than usual and they spilled enticingly over the new two-piece lacy outfit.

"So you approve, I see," Cory smiled. Adrian shook his head eagerly up and down. "Well, that's good. Because it's all for you, baby."

Adrian grinned. "Damn, when did I ever get so lucky?"

"Since the day you met me, I suppose," Cory answered his question. She proceeded to sit on his lap. "So are you busy . . . I got some dessert for you?" she asked, slowly gyrating her hips.

"Not anymore," he anxiously responded. "Just give me a minute to log out here, ma'am. And I'll be right with ya."

Cory giggled. "So, what were you really doing in here all this time?" she asked.

"Just playing around. Nothing important," he answered hastily. Adrian was about to close the window on his program when Cory quickly stopped him.

"Wait! What's this, baby?" she asked.

"This? Just a little something I was working on," he replied.

"But why does it look like a bunch of crazy stuff? It looks like Greek," Cory laughed.

"That's because it's coding for the programming language I was working with," Adrian responded. "It's not Greek. It's called Java."

"So . . . what are you using it for?"

"I'm trying to create a computer game actually," Adrian answered her question nonchalantly.

"Wait. Hold up! Baby, since when did you know about coding and programming languages and creating computer games?" Cory asked, bewildered.

Adrian laughed out, "Let me see. Since I have a first degree in IT."

Cory's mouth opened wide. "Adrian, you have a degree in information technology?"

"Yep. I got it when I was in the Marines. I studied IT for four years when I enlisted."

"And how come you never told me something as important as this?"

"I didn't know this was so important to you. A degree that is," Adrian offered.

"Of course this is important to me."

"There you go. It's important to you. Degrees don't define who I am, Cory."

"But my point is that you had a degree all this time and you never once said anything to me about it, Adrian."

"Because it never came up, baby, that's why. Look, could you stop getting all worked up over this whole degree thing. I think I have something much better for you to get all worked up on right here," he flashed her a devilish smile. Adrian placed Cory's hand on his rock-hard erection. "See how much I like your pretty little outfit," he said, nibbling her ear.

Cory immediately removed her hand from the spot. "Adrian, but I want to know everything about you."

"In time, baby. You'll get to know everything," he assured her.

"But I can't help but wonder now what other little secrets you have up your sleeves," Cory remarked out of nowhere.

*

Cory's comment took Adrian by surprise. He stopped his nibbling. He tensed. In fact, every muscle in his body tensed. He immediately lost his erection. How was he supposed to answer that? He knew the day would come sooner or later. But this was too soon. They were only married three months now.

All of a sudden, the voice in his head returned, urging him to tell her. He had to tell Cory everything. It was about time he told her this. Tonight.

"Maybe there's something else I need to tell you, Cory."

"I'm listening," she prodded him.

"Okay, where do I begin?" he started. Adrian was searching for the right words. "This happened a while back when we didn't even know each other yet. . . . " Adrian suddenly trailed off. His cell phone buzzing on the desk was interrupting him. He picked it up and looked at the flashing screen.

He knew his drill. It was late at night so he would only take this call if it were his mother or sister calling. It was Anna and her immaculate timing as usual! "Baby, I got to take this. It's Anna," he said to Cory.

"Okay. I'll be waiting in the bedroom," Cory announced as she got up off his lap. "Don't be too long. I never did a *techie* before," she grinned as she ran her fingers along the hardness of his chest. "Tell Anna I said hi."

Adrian smiled at her confession. When he answered, Anna wasted no time and proceeded to tell him all about this new guy she met and was seeing. She wanted him and Cory to double-date with them so that Adrian could drill the guy and check him out.

When he ended the conversation, it took him a few moments to regroup his train of thought of what he was actually going to say to Cory. He turned off his laptop and headed for their bedroom.

Cory was lying on the bed when Adrian entered. She looked like she was asleep, her hair spread about the pillow. He probably took longer than he had expected on the phone but talking to Anna at least got his mind away from the task at hand, if only for a little while, anyway. He was trying to explain to her all the reasons why he was not going to use his military training to figure out her date for her. That was something she needed to do on her own.

"Cory?" Adrian played with her cheek. "Baby, are you really asleep?" he asked. Cory wasn't budging. She must have fallen asleep waiting for him to join her. "Baby, I have something important to tell you." Still no response from her. She was out like a light. Adrian pulled the sheets over her shoulders and kissed her.

If he truly didn't love this woman sleeping next to him, Adrian would be lying to himself. Maybe it was a good sign she fell asleep he told himself. But Adrian couldn't sleep that night. His eyes remained wide open. He couldn't imagine what would happen when he did tell her. How would she react? Would this be the end to his now-perfect life?

Chapter 25

She looked up in surprise from the presentation she was working on when Adrian casually strolled into the bedroom. She must have been seriously concentrating on her work because she hadn't heard him come into the apartment at all. Then again, Cory wasn't expecting to see him strolling in here at midday. He wasn't expected till tomorrow morning, as was the norm.

Both she and her jade green laptop were perched in the middle of the huge bed. They had been there the entire morning. Cory had to finish this in time for an early Monday morning video conference from Spain. It was a PowerPoint synopsis of all the company's outreach initiatives for the past six months.

They were already two weeks behind on it, all the more reason why it suddenly became her job. But Cory felt proud doing it because it only proved that she did work for a socially responsible company that cared about its surrounding communities.

Since it was Friday and her day off, Cory decided she'd work assiduously on it from home. Also, Adrian wouldn't be around to distract her either. Even though he was such an amazingly sweet distraction, it seemed like every time they were alone together they were constantly at it.

She was hell-bent and intent on finishing this task today because of the plans she had in-store for him over the weekend. Cory planned on surprising him with an early morning trip to Maracas, the most popular beach on the island. They both needed a day of relaxation after a very demanding work week. Then it would be time to model lingerie for her eager audience of one when they got home.

Remembering the last time they had been to the beach brought a smile to Cory's lips. The sun was dipping below the horizon for the evening. The beach was quiet and secluded. She had wrapped her legs around Adrian's waist as they weaved and bobbed in the incoming tide surges. And all it took was one kiss in the water.

She could still taste the saltiness of the ocean against Adrian's lips. Maybe it was the sea, erotically caressing their scantily clad bodies or the natural beauty of their surroundings with the setting sun but it had been so difficult for them both to resist each other then. As the heat of their already entwined bodies became too much to bear, they both succumbed to their guilty pleasures right there in the ocean. It was a perfect end to a beautiful honeymoon for them.

Cory was shocked to see him now. "Adrian? What're you doing here?" She immediately saved all the recent additions of her presentation onto her flash drive inserted in the laptop.

"Hey, baby. Something came up," was Adrian's response. He sat on the bed next to her and immediately began undressing.

Cory pushed aside the laptop, forgetting all about her work for a while. "Well, what is it?"

"Remember when I told you sometimes we may have to pursue wanted men who are on the run or hiding out in the forests, etcetera?"

"Yes?"

"Well, we just got a mission to do that. There's a guy on the run wanted in connection for the murders of his wife and two children."

"What? But where?"

"Deep south."

"Oh, yeah, I think I heard Anna reading that story last night. The police held him for domestic violence and after he threatened to kill his wife and then he escaped police custody. So how long will you all take to find him you think?"

"We can't be certain but I'm hoping two days max."

"Two days?" Cory asked in total disbelief.

"Yeah. I'm sorry, Cory, but I was mandated to lead this exercise. You know soldiers lead when it's in the forest. That's one of our areas of expertise," he explained. She started getting off the bed.

"Baby, where're you going?" Adrian asked, now taking his boots off.

"I can't believe it. These criminals are ruining my love life," Cory announced. So much for her weekend plans now.

"But I'll be back before you know it." Adrian laughed. "Come here, baby." It sounded like a command coming from Adrian.

"No!"

"Okay. Then I'll just have to come over there and get you myself." Adrian calmly crossed the bedroom floor. He was now bare-chested and stripped down to his boxers. Resting both hands up against the door and towering above her, the taut muscles of his chest and arms looking more pronounced than ever, Adrian stared down at her. "Cory, are you going to fight me on this?"

"No," she calmly replied this time, changing her tone.

Without touching anywhere else on her body, he kissed her on her neck. "Good. Now, do you want me to beg you, is that it?" he whispered, nibbling her ear. "Because I can beg you if you want, Cory."

"No! I have a presentation to finish, Adrian," she blurted out, noticing his swelling erection.

Adrian kissed her on her lips, his hotness silencing her and still the only thing touching her body. He moved down to her cleavage, showering feather-light kisses along the top of her breasts.

Cory inhaled sharply. All it took was one look, one touch, one kiss from him to drive her totally insane. *Why God, did this man have to be so damn sexy?*

"Didn't you get enough of this, this morning?" she asked.

"I did. But that was breakfast. It's now lunch and I'm starving again. So what will it be, baby?" Adrian continued to tease her.

Cory groaned out aloud, "I think you need to stop this."

Completely ignoring her, Adrian knelt down and showered soft kisses along her bare legs. When his lips reached the edge of the short denim skirt she was wearing, he paused. "Did I ever tell you, you have the most gorgeous legs I ever saw?"

"Yes, you_did," she squirmed. Adrian allowed his hands to freely roam upwards, caressing her inner thighs. Cory was trying her hardest but a soft moan still managed to escape her lips.

"Well, I feel like I always have to stop and appreciate beauty when I see it. And since you're having so much fun, may I remove these?" He was referring to her thong underwear.

The last remnants of Cory's resolve instantaneously melted away. She closed her eyes. "Yes." It was more of a breathless whisper coming from her.

Adrian smiled. "I didn't hear you, baby."

"*Si, por favor.*" Cory said this much louder and with urgency in her voice.

"Damn, you sound so sexy rattling off Spanish. You know that?"

"*Si,*" she giggled this time.

Adrian swiftly removed her panties. Now he was free to work his magic. He hiked up her skirt around her waist.

"Urrr . . . I hate you for making me want you so much," Cory complained but grabbed his head, urgently pulling him to her heated center. Adrian's tongue delved into her sweetness, never disappointing her. "Oooh," she crooned as she gyrated against the door.

"Do you like that, baby?" Adrian asked.

"No!" she lied.

"Liar! Tell me," Adrian commanded. This time, he was more forceful with her, his hot slippery tongue hungrily enjoying its meal.

"Oh God, I love you so much," Cory eventually screamed out.

"So . . . should I take that as a yes, then?" He grinned. Adrian knew exactly what he was doing to her.

"Yes," Cory laughed. "You know I absolutely love it when you do that."

With that Adrian lifted her and flung her effortlessly over his broad shoulders. Cory shrieked and giggled as he took her over to the bed and laid her down. "And I absolutely love to be inside of you," he remarked.

"Yes, but my turn to be on top this time," she insisted.

"Fine with me." Adrian flipped positions with her on the bed so that Cory was now sitting seductively on his muscular thighs, her legs spread-eagled on either side of him. His eyes looked appreciative as she flashed him.

"So how much time do we have?"

"About one hour," Adrian replied after consulting his watch.

Cory hurriedly removed his underwear before she complained, "That's it? What're we going to do in an hour, Adrian?"

"A lot. If only you'd stop talking and stop trying to resist me, woman."

"Fine," Cory huffed. Adrian willingly helped her get her camisole over her head. When her bare breasts were revealed, his hands automatically moved up to cup them.

"Oh and by the way, lieutenant. When I'm done with you in one hour, you'll never want to go into the forests again."

"Is that so? What, are you threatening me now, Cory?" Adrian stopped his caressing to jokingly ask her.

"No. I'm promising you."

"Well, I don't think I can complain 'bout that, baby," he laughed.

"Oh, you won't be complaining," Cory explained as she turned her entire body in the opposite direction. She looked back at him flashing a naughty grin as she started moving her body, sensuously gyrating her hips down on his eager shaft.

"Oh . . . shit!" Adrian exclaimed. His hands now moved to cup her firm behind.

"So do you like that, baby?" Cory asked.

"Oh, hell yeah!"

Their lovemaking was nothing short of spectacular for the short space of time they had together. Yet, it felt like they had all the time in the world. After she enjoyed giving him what she called the "island workout of his life," Cory quickly surrendered to Adrian in sweet abandon, only then allowing him to take total possession of her body. They left the bed and were making wild, passionate love against the wall, against the door, anywhere that had a stable backing.

"Cory!" Adrian called her name breathlessly. Her legs were wrapped tightly around his waist, her nails sinking into his flesh as he repeatedly drilled into her against the closet. He exploded when she screamed his name, too, causing them both to climax.

After a couple more orgasms like that, Cory must have dozed off. She was physically exhausted after their bout of loving now and from earlier this morning. When she stirred on the bed, Adrian had already showered and changed into fresh military fatigues. Her mind momentarily flashed back to just a few hours ago. Cory had woken before him and proceeded to jump his bones. Adrian awoke to some early morning action between the sheets. She didn't want her purchase to go to waste so they picked up where they left off last night. Even though it was at five in the morning, Cory had worked that lingerie, blowing his mind over and over in it.

"Hey, sleepy head." He was strapping back his pistol into the holster on his leg.

"Hey," Cory responded groggily. "When did I fall asleep?"

"Probably just as soon as I was finished with you," Adrian grinned, buttoning up his camouflage jacket. "So hopefully that would be sufficient to last you two days, right?"

"Mmmm," Cory smiled. "I'll miss you so much, baby."

"Don't worry. I'll try my best to get this guy as quickly as possible . . . for your sake."

"I sure hope so."

Adrian sat on the bed and tried but in vain to smooth her hair back. He kissed her gently.

"Get some rest, baby. And Cory . . . be good till I get back."

"I'll try my very best," she groaned when Adrian started heading for the door. "Adrian, wait!"

He stopped just as he was about to turn the lock.

"You were saying to me last night that you had something to tell me. You started but then your phone rang with Anna and then I fell asleep I think," Cory was saying. "So what was it?"

Adrian's body tensed. "Baby, it's a long story. I'll tell you when I get back, okay?"

"You promise?"

"Yep. Boy Scouts honor. Soon as I get back."

Cory smiled as Adrian blew her a kiss and opened the door to leave. She wondered what his story was. She couldn't imagine Adrian doing anything crazy, other than what she supposed came with being in the military. So she knew it couldn't be anything like that. Her next guess was an affair. It couldn't have been that either she reasoned. Cory knew by the time she was finished with him, he didn't have the strength to satisfy another woman. Besides, he loved her too much. He would never do anything to hurt her. But whatever it was would have to wait till he got back.

When Cory heard the front door closing, it signaled the first time since being married to Adrian that she wasn't going to see him for two entire long days.

Chapter 26

Cory remained glued to the bed for a while longer after Adrian left, daydreaming again. She was thinking about their life together. How much she loved him and how much he loved her. She had no idea where she would have been without him in her life but she felt definitely blessed to have him there.

"Okay, Cory. It's time to get back to work," she scolded herself out loud. She got off the bed and searched around for her clothes. It was amazing how fast it would always come off when Adrian was around. That was when she noticed it. Her laptop lay on the floor, half hidden under the bed. Horror immediately flashed across her face.

Please tell me nothing's wrong with it, played in Cory's mind over and over like a broken record. *Please, please, please,* she begged. It was probably knocked over during their just concluded, rather adventurous lovemaking session. But neither of them had been bothered by this possibility whilst getting busy a short while ago.

Cory picked up the laptop off the floor and screamed. "Oh, no!" Tears were already welling in her eyes. The top of it was busted and had one long crack running along its entire surface. She immediately opened it and pressed the power button. Nothing happened. It wasn't powering up. It wasn't working. Panic finally set in.

How the hell was she going to finish her presentation now? *Think Cory, think.* She decided to call Adrian. He would know what to do. After all, he was the IT major in college. A fact she only found out last night for that matter. But a fact she more than appreciated at this moment, however.

Cory dialed Adrian's number. After only two rings, he answered, "Hey, gorgeous. Missing me, already?"

"Yes, I am," Cory hastily answered. "Unfortunately, that's not the reason why I'm calling you."

"What is it, baby? Everything okay?" Adrian's tone immediately changed from one of flirting to one of concern.

"No, everything is not okay. Adrian, my laptop is broken," Cory cried into the phone. "It fell from the bed to the floor. And now it's all cracked up and not coming on when I tried the power button. It isn't getting any power, Adrian. And I have to finish this presentation today. What am I going to do?"

"Baby, calm down," Adrian demanded. "Look, if the screen is cracked you wouldn't be able to see anything, anyway. Were you able to save any of your work?"

"Yes, my flash is still connected."

"Well, okay. At least you have something. All you need is a new machine, then. Why don't you use my laptop?"

"That's a great idea." Cory prayed her flash wasn't damaged from the fall, too; otherwise she would have to start from scratch and redo the entire thing and all her hard work would have been but in vain. "What would I ever do without you, baby?"

"Don't know. Now get cracking. You have work to do," Adrian commanded.

"Oh and by the way lieutenant, you owe me a new laptop."

"So it's my entire fault now, is that it?" Adrian joked.

"Yes. You're the one who wanted to make love when I had work to do," Cory retorted.

"Like you didn't . . . besides, I didn't hear you complaining, baby," Adrian laughed.

"Bye, baby," Cory laughed and ended the call.

She went into the second bedroom Adrian had converted into his study and opened up his laptop. When the screen came up, it demanded a password code to be entered.

"Dammit," Cory cursed. She didn't know Adrian's password for his laptop because she'd never used it before now. She would just have to call him again.

"Adrian, sorry to bother you again but I need to get your

password please."

"Oh yeah, I forgot about that. It's Marine One. With a capital M and capital O."

"Marine One? Why am I not surprised?" Cory typed in the password. "Great, it worked. Thanks, baby."

"Talk to ya later," Adrian said and hung up.

Now, she was way behind but she wasn't going to stop until she finished the damn thing this time. Cory inserted her flash drive into Adrian's laptop. She breathed a sigh of relief when it was recognized. She was able to download all of the presentation she had completed so far onto his laptop so she could work from there. And she worked nonstop for the next three hours until she was finished, finally.

She checked and double-checked the PowerPoint. She checked for grammar and spelling. She vetted it for easy navigability and pleasing use of graphics. She ensured the colors she used were easy on the eyes. When she was finally satisfied that everything was okay with her presentation, she e-mailed it to Javier and Danielle. They would have it to look over as soon as they got in on Monday morning to prep themselves before the meeting started.

"Finally," Cory shrieked elatedly. Now, she could concentrate on relaxing for the rest of the weekend. Take a long soak in the tub, pour herself a glass of wine, or even look at a movie.

She was about to shut down when she decided to send her presentation to Adrian's recycle bin first. It was quite a large file and she didn't want it taking up too much memory on his laptop. He was working on his computer game, which probably took up a whole lot of memory in itself. Cory deleted the presentation from the documents window and clicked on the recycle bin to empty it from there, too.

As she was about to delete it, something caught her attention. There was another file in the recycle bin. It read: Report - Confidential. Cory held her hand. Her mind started racing. She thought about it for a moment. What could Adrian possibly have in this confidential file? And what was it doing in his recycle bin?

Probably his work stuff, Cory decided. Adrian's job entailed a lot of challenges and Lord knows what else Cory knew. But he always spared her the details, never speaking about it. Maybe this file might give her some clues as to what he really did on the job. Curiosity got the better of her. Cory wanted to know what was in that file. She restored the file, double-clicked on the folder to open it up and saw one single item in it.

A word document named Report opened up. It was in a letter format addressed to the Commissioner and carbon copied to the Brigadier and Minister. It was dated two years ago. The caption read: Report on Shooting Incident and the date. The 3rd of March? Why was that date so familiar to her? Cory read the document:

Dear Sirs,

As instructed by you, I, Second Lieutenant Adrian Mendez, hereby truthfully give my account of the events leading up to the shooting deaths of Patrick Morris, Anthony Powell, Marlon Williams and Collin Phillips on the night of March 3.

Cory froze. Her eyes remained glued to the screen. *Collin Phillips?* Maybe she didn't see correctly. She read it over. Good, she wasn't delusional. It was indeed Collin Phillips she saw. The date was also correct, but that was the date Collin was killed. What was Adrian doing with this document? He didn't know about Collin or how he was killed. She had only told him about this the night he had dinner over at her house.

She continued reading the second paragraph. It stated the names and ranks of seven other soldiers and officers who were in the company of Adrian on patrol in the city that night. The third paragraph gave details of the APB they received but it was when Cory reached the fourth paragraph that she stopped. That part read:

After all rounds stopped firing and all went quiet, I proceeded to firstly check on the driver of the vehicle as he was the one closest to my position. He was slumped behind the wheel. I checked for a pulse on his neck. There was none. It was then I realized he was already dead on the scene. This was later confirmed by homicide officers who immediately arrived. The driver of the vehicle was later identified as Collin Phillips. He wasn't a known felon to the police. He wasn't armed.

Her body trembled. There was a pain in her chest, constricting her heart's ability to pump her blood. Panic gripped her. Fear shot through her. A muffled sound caught in her throat but it sounded too weird to be a scream. Between the blinding hot tears, Cory read the part over. Could this really be *her* Collin? The names, the date, the time, and the events were all familiar to her. This couldn't be possible, still? How could Adrian have been there? He wouldn't know about something like this and keep it from her, would he?

Cory glided off the chair and sank to the floor, clutching her chest. It all began coming at her at once. Adrian's job. He killed for a living. He never wanted to speak to her about how many people he had actually killed. His unexpected marriage proposal on the fort that day. Their wedding in Tobago. His undivided attention to all her needs these past three months. How happy she was. His IT degree and other dark secrets he probably kept from her. Her father's reaction to his career choice. And now this.

"Oh, God!" Cory thought of her father now. He had been so right after all. Why hadn't she listened to him? How could she ever face him again? He would never forgive her for this.

Cory instantly remembered the days just after Collin's death. She was still trying to come to terms with her mother's breast cancer diagnosis. Then, her mother went soon after Collin. Everyone had said it was because of the grief. She had just given up and didn't care to live anymore.

This had been the most dreadful time in her life. Many times she just wanted to die herself. Then her emotional breakdown quickly followed brought on by the post traumatic stress of their deaths.

She couldn't eat or sleep. She had to be treated by medication to get over this. If she hadn't been treated, she may have very well been admitted to a psychiatric ward by now. Then during all this came the break-up with Preston.

And all of this was because of Adrian? If it wasn't for him, her brother and mother would still be alive today. How could Adrian do this to her, after he claimed to love her? It was all a lie. Everything was a lie from the beginning. The life she had now was a lie.

Was this all a big game for him? How long did he think he could fool her for? For her entire life? Till she was dead, too? No wonder she found this report in his recycle bin. Adrian had no intention of her ever finding out about it. But how could he have been so careless as to leave it there without deleting it forever? That was his big mistake.

"You're such a fool, Cory!" she screamed at herself. "To think this man could really love you."

She didn't know how long she remained sobbing on the floor. She only got up because her throat was all dried out. She passed the bathroom on her way to the kitchen. When she looked in the mirror, she jumped at the scary reflection staring back at her. Her eyes were red and bloodshot, puffy and swollen in her tear-stained face. Her hair didn't make things any better either, falling in a mess about her troubled facial features.

In the kitchen, she needed that drink of wine now but there was none anywhere. She couldn't believe she was out of wine. She needed something strong and water wasn't an option this time. Cory frantically searched through the kitchen cupboards for something. Anything. All she eventually found was a bottle of scotch. She didn't drink scotch, but scotch would have to do today. She cracked the new seal on the bottle and poured a half glass of the amber-colored liquid.

She took a deep breath and downed the entire thing in one

go. The fiery liquid stung her throat and pained her as it went down. She coughed and beat against her chest to ease the initial discomfort. That wasn't too bad. At least it was better than this ridiculous predicament she was in now. Two more half glasses of scotch later and her anger was at a boiling point, steaming through her entire body. Cory needed to know how and why Adrian could do such a thing to her.

She dialed his cell phone for the third time for the day.

*

"Hi, baby. Can I call you back in a minute?" Adrian immediately answered.

"No, you may not."

"Cory? What's wrong?"

"Are you still at the base?" she asked quietly. Coldly.

"Yes. We're getting ready to move out in a little bit. What's wrong? Why're you sounding like that? You sound so distant."

"I need you to come home."

"What? When?"

"Now!" Cory shouted at him.

"Cory, but I can't. C'mon, you know I can't do that now, baby," Adrian pleaded with her. "Cory, are you going to tell me what's wrong? Are you feeling okay?"

"No, I'm not okay," Cory screamed.

"Well, then tell me what's wrong, Cory," Adrian found his own voice rising from the anticipation he was starting to feel.

"Everything."

"God, Cory! Just talk to me." There was another long silence. "Cory . . . just stay where you are. I'll be there shortly."

Adrian turned his attention back to the man with the expectant look on his face sitting across from him in his office. They were going over the last-minute details of the search together. Since his return to base that afternoon, they were either in meetings, preparing for the exercise, or loading their weapons, food, and camping gear into the vehicles.

"Major, I need to be excused, sir. There's an emergency at my home that I need to investigate now."

"Mendez, can't anybody else look into that for you?" Major Benjamin asked him.

"No," Adrian simply replied. "It's my wife, sir."

"Well, we're moving out at 1800 hours. And you have to lead this exercise. Half an hour is all you have and that's it, Mendez."

"Roger that, major."

"Allyuh young men need to learn how to handle your women when duty calls."

Obviously, Major Benjamin didn't know *his* woman. Cory was one firecracker he did not want to mess with. When he left his office, Adrian immediately summoned two of his armed soldiers to accompany him to his apartment. He didn't know what to expect there.

All he knew was that he didn't like the way Cory was sounding over the phone. She wasn't exactly talking to him either. Or could she even talk? Adrian's mind began to race. Was there somebody else with her? Was she under some sort of threat? Was she being coerced? If anyone dare hurt his wife and he found them, make no mistake, he knew what he'd do to them.

"Step on it, man," Adrian ordered the soldier who was driving. "I only have half hour."

"Jus' say the word, LT." The soldier really stepped on it because he pulled up at Adrian's apartment building only a few minutes later. Adrian practically flew out and bounded toward the elevator. The front door was locked as usual. There wasn't anybody suspiciously lurking around the corridor. Everything looked in order to him. Adrian drew the gun strapped on his leg just in case.

Chapter 27

Nothing prepared Adrian for what met his eyes when he unlocked the front door of his apartment. His heart immediately plunged in his chest. Cory was sitting in the darkened living room, looking all dazed. She didn't get up to greet him. Adrian's trained eyes quickly darted around the room searching for anyone else who might be there with her.

Then he noticed the opened bottle of scotch on the coffee table in front of her. Was she drunk? What the hell was she thinking? Making him think the worst that someone was probably here attacking her and here she was getting herself wasted. Having him rush over here, jeopardizing his duties like that.

Relief washed over him first. Cory was all right. He strapped his gun back in its place. "Cory, since when do you drink scotch by the way?" Adrian asked in a low voice. "You hate scotch," he added. There was no answer.

He switched on the lights. Cory winced. Then Adrian noticed the state of her face. Swollen, red and puffy. He immediately rushed toward her, fearing the worst. "Cory what happened?" Adrian barked at her, demanding a real answer from her this time.

A smile played on her lips now. "Tell me again why you married me, Adrian," she demanded quietly.

"*What?*" Adrian demanded. "Please tell me this is not the reason you had me rush over here."

"No! You tell me!" she screamed at him. "I need to know why."

"Cory, I don't have to tell you because you already know why. I tell you every day, for Pete's sake!"

"But I need to hear it now."

Adrian took a deep breath and sat down next to her on the sofa. Softening his tone he said, "Because I love you, Cory. Is that what you wanted to hear?"

Cory burst into hysterical laughter. "*You* love me?" she asked him incredulously. "Then how is it possible for a man who claims he loves me to do such an evil thing like this to me?"

Adrian was feeling something rising in his chest. That sickening feeling was coming back. "Cory, what're you talking about?" His voice was back to its normal low tone again.

"*This* is what I'm talking about, Adrian," she yelled as she flung sheets of paper at him. Adrian caught a page, read the top, immediately added up the events, and went cold.

"God, Cory! I'm so sorry. You weren't supposed to find out like this," Adrian said.

"Well, I suppose you should be more careful with the information you have stored on your laptop. Especially when you allow other people to use it."

"Cory, I'm sorry. Baby, I swear. I was going to tell you everything. This was what I was going to tell you last night," Adrian tried to explain.

"Sure you were. Boy Scouts honor, right?" Cory laughed. "You know, I thought you were an honorable man, Adrian. But you're just like the rest of them. You're such a liar!"

"Cory, I never once lied to you."

"So what do you call this, then? Lying by omission is still lying, Adrian. You knew about this all the while and was stringing me all along like a fool."

"Cory, that's not what happened. Look, I need to explain everything to you and exactly the way it all happened that night."

"No! You had six months to tell me everything, Adrian. *Six months!*" Cory shrieked. "I don't want to hear anything now."

"But I only found out about this the night I had dinner at your house, I swear to you. When you showed me that photo of you and Collin, that's when everything clicked."

"Liar!" Cory shouted to his face.

"That's the truth, Cory."

Cory went quiet for a while. "So that's the reason why I didn't see you for days after that? That's why you couldn't return any of my calls? Then you made up a lame work excuse thing and then you supposedly popped the question you thought I wanted to hear. You were planning your strategy all along?" Cory asked dumbfounded. When Adrian didn't answer her question or say anything, she quietly began to sob.

"Oh my God. I was such a fool. To think you loved me and wanted to marry me, Adrian. When all you really wanted to do was to cover your ass. So that I'd never find out what you did. How could you do this to me?" Cory managed between the sobs. "After you made love to me this morning and this afternoon. After you look me in my face everyday, Adrian? How could you do this?"

"Baby, no! That's not true. I love you more than life itself, Cory and I wanted to marry you. I couldn't live my life without you in it." Adrian was becoming desperate for Cory to understand what he was trying to say to her. He took her hands into his. "You have to believe me, Cory."

Cory screamed and pushed his hands away from hers. "How could I ever believe anything you have to say to me again, Adrian?"

"You have to believe me, Cory. Trust me, I'll never do anything to intentionally hurt you, baby."

"Only you did, Adrian," she yelled. "You killed my brother. And you pretended to love me to cover it up. You lied to me. And now you want me to trust you?"

"Cory, your brother's killing was an accident," Adrian barked at her.

"So tell me. Since you were the closest to Collin, how many of your bullets you think went into him?"

"Surely, you don't expect me to answer that, Cory."

"Tell me!" she screamed at him again.

"I don't know!" Adrian screamed back at her.

"You're nothing but a murderer, Adrian," Cory looked him in the eye when she quietly said this to his face. "You killed my brother and you killed my mother."

Her words stung Adrian like a slap in the face. He never expected to hear these words coming from Cory, of all people. They could have come from anybody else. But not her.

His heart squeezed against his rib cage. Adrian suddenly felt ashamed. But nothing could come to his mind to say to her. Nothing. Because she was right. So much for the honor and courage he so prided in himself.

"I'll take full responsibility for your brother's death, Cory. But your mother died from breast cancer," Adrian said quietly.

"No! She died because you killed her firstborn son and she didn't want to live anymore, Adrian," Cory shouted.

Adrian came closer to her, trying to comfort her in his arms but Cory wasn't having any of it.

"Don't touch me!"

A knock on the door shifted Adrian's attention from Cory for the first time since he'd come home. He waited till he heard the knock again. "We aren't finished yet, Cory," he quietly said to her as he got up to get the door. When he opened it, one of the soldiers who accompanied him was standing outside.

"Is everything okay, LT?" he asked.

"Everything is fine, soldier," he replied.

"Then, sir, with all due respect, we have to get back to base."

"Just give me a minute," Adrian said to him and closed the door.

When he turned around, Cory wasn't sitting on the sofa anymore. He headed straight for the bedroom. He turned the door handle but it was locked. Adrian began banging on the door, begging Cory to let him in. "Baby, please open the door. We haven't finished talking about this."

"I don't want to talk anymore, Adrian. I'm tired," Cory shouted from behind the door.

"Cory, c'mon." Adrian could have easily broken the door in but he knew that would only serve to scare Cory even further. She was already in such a delicate, fragile state right now. He was such a fool. He never prepared himself for this day. He never imagined all this drama. But what did he expect? He drove her to this state. Adrian was mad as hell with himself for not telling Cory as soon as he realized everything. Maybe all of this heartache could have been avoided.

"Cory, I have to go," Adrian at last said through the closed door. "When I get back, we need to really talk about this, okay." Adrian didn't want to go. But he really had to go now.

"Yeah, I know you have to go, Adrian. So just go, then. National duty is calling," Cory scathingly said.

Adrian shook his head in despair as he continued to press his body against the door. "I know I should've told you this before . . . but Cory I didn't want to lose you. I know I was selfish and I'm so sorry, baby. I know I'm not perfect. Please promise me when I get back we'll talk some more about this." But there was only silence on the other side of the door now.

Chapter 28

Cory immediately started packing when she heard the front door lock behind Adrian. He was gone now and she absolutely knew she couldn't stay here any minute longer. No way was she going to sit around and wait two whole days for Adrian to return home. To tell her what? She already heard more than enough from him. She had to get out of here. Out of his apartment. Out of town. Out of this island. Anywhere but here. It was just too painful to stay.

Cory couldn't understand how one minute you could be so in love with someone and then in the next want to get as far away from them as you could. But where could she go? Who could she turn to now? She certainly couldn't go home to her father after this. Not with everything that just happened. In fact, how could she ever look him in his face again after what Adrian did to her family?

She didn't want to bother her girlfriends with this, either. There was one person left she knew she could always count on. She dialed Jay's number and asked him a favor. To take her to the airport. She needed to get off this island immediately. In half an hour's time, Jay pulled up outside the gate. She hastily threw on a pair of dark blue skinny jeans and a yellow tank top. No wonder they were called skinny jeans. Cory had to really wiggle her way into them to get them up and over her wide hips and big butt. But she was too depressed right now to even think about her weight gain.

Depressed was an understatement. She was heartbroken. She was angry, too, but more so with herself for being so idiotic as to put herself once again in this position because of a damn man. Not just any man but the love of her life, she reminded herself. She slipped some sandals on her feet and a dab of lip gloss in the mirror and she was all ready. Not forgetting her sunglasses, Cory slipped on her darkest pair.

She hastily threw her luggage in the back seat. It was now a little after six in the evening and the sun was setting. Depending on the traffic situation, they should be in the airport about one hour from now, Cory hopefully estimated.

"What's up with the sunglasses?" Jay immediately asked her as she got into the front passenger's seat beside him.

"Don't ask, okay," Cory shot back. "People do wear them at night time by the way."

"Only if you're Usher Raymond," Jay said as he started the car.

When they were finally on their way, he asked her, "So what's really going on, Cory?"

"Nothing!"

"Is your grandmother sick or something? Why're you rushing over to Tobago so suddenly?" Jay pressed her. "You don't look too good yourself, Ri-Ri."

"Did anybody ever tell you how annoying you are sometimes? I'm fine, okay. I just need to see my grandmother, that's all."

"Look, how long have we known each other, eh? Five long years," he continued. "Talk to me, Cory. I've been around you for too long to know when something's wrong."

"Look, it doesn't matter how long you know someone for, okay. You still may not know that person," Cory snapped at him. "You'll still get screwed in the end."

"Well, I'm sorry for asking."

Cory softened somewhat. "Look, Jay, I'm sorry for snapping at you but I really don't feel like talking right now."

"Fine, Cory."

For the remainder of the drive there was no conversation in the car, only Jay's annoying and out-of-key singing along to every damn song playing on the radio. Trying his best to annoy her further, no doubt, but Cory was too deep in her own thoughts to even care. She stared through the window, pondering her future and what she was going to do. She didn't have a clue or clear solution to this mess. It's not everyday you find out your husband killed your brother in the line of duty.

When Jay finally pulled up at the airport, he started to get out the car to help her with her luggage. Cory immediately stopped him.

"Jay, thank you so much for this," she said to him. She really meant it. "I'll be fine, don't worry. You can go ahead. I'll just go in and buy a ticket and wait, okay."

"Are you sure, Cory?" he asked. "Because I don't want to have to answer that husband of yours if you go missing or something."

She smiled. Cory knew Jay was a bit wary of Adrian, due to the mere fact that he was always armed. "I wouldn't worry about him if I were you." Cory waved to him and closed the door of his car.

"What do you mean by that, Cory?" Jay shouted after her.

She didn't even bother to give him an answer or explanation for that matter, as she pulled out the handle of her traveling bag and wheeled it hurriedly through the automatic doors of the airport.

It was the middle of July and the peak of the summer vacation. School was out so everyone was busy traveling between the two islands or the Caribbean and North America. Cory had forgotten all about the mayhem at the airport during this time of year. The place was bursting at its seams with people. Luggage was strewn everywhere and children were running and screaming all over the place. A group of them almost ran her over as she wheeled her lone bag in.

Cory joined a line and waited for her turn to go up to the counter. "Hi. I need a ticket to go to Tobago, please," she said to the girl behind the counter. She had been screaming at the top of her voice with Adrian and crying her eyeballs out all evening so she was now going hoarse.

Thankfully, she was able to get a ticket but on the last flight out for the night. This wasn't until 10:00 so she had another two hours or so before boarding the plane. Cory decided to call her grandmother and tell her she was coming over tonight. Then she'd go buy some dinner and something to read perhaps. She didn't want to even think about Adrian anymore.

*

All Adrian wanted to do was to find this murderer on the run as quickly as possible and get back home to Cory. He had to go back and make her understand. He had to explain her everything.

Adrian hardly said anything for the entire two-hour-long drive to the south of the island. He stared at nothing in particular as the constant chatter of the others continued around him. He could only think about Cory. He never saw her looking so hysterical before. He hated seeing her cry or seeing her so unhappy. And to know that it was all his doing was just too much for Adrian to bear.

When the group of them was dropped off, they gathered their gear and started making their way through the dark forests. Adrian was leading this mission and he didn't have any time to waste. He had to get this exercise completed successfully and as quickly as possible, then be on his way home. It was hard enough for him to concentrate on what he had to do to lead his team because he regretted not being with Cory, to comfort her.

For the very first time, he didn't feel like being here or leading this mission. After the long trek further into the forests, when they finally stopped to set up their camp for the night, it was close to midnight. Several of the men were complaining about Adrian's hectic pace Though he too was physically and emotionally drained, he couldn't sleep a wink.

*

It was after eleven in the night when Cory's taxi finally pulled up in front her grandmother's house. She was physically exhausted and mentally drained. She had silently sat and cried for the entire twenty-minute flight over here. Thankfully, she had gotten a window seat so she just stared out into the blackness and cried her heart out.

Just this afternoon she was so happy. She felt so complete. Now, within a few hours, her world was turned upside down, all because of a stupid document she read. Cory blamed herself at first. She had no right to go snooping into Adrian's private stuff. She should have trusted him and left it at that. But no! She had to play Curious George and read the damn thing.

Her grandmother was waiting up for her. When she opened the front door, concern and happiness were both etched on her aging face.

"Hi, Gran," Cory tried her best to beam at her grandmother. She was still wearing her sunglasses when she entered the house.

"Hi, sugar." Her grandmother gave her a long, tight squeeze. This felt so amazingly warm and genuine that it only caused Cory to start sobbing again.

"What's the matter, sugar? Why're you crying?"

"Oh, nothing, Gran. I'm just so happy to see you, that's all. I haven't seen you since the wedding, remember?"

Cory immediately changed the subject. "I love the new hair color, Gran. Purple looks good on you," she laughed for the first time since earlier in the afternoon.

"Oh, this is a big mistake, love. My regular hairdresser was sick but I was desperate because I had this wedding to attend. So I had this new trainee color my hair for me. And this was the result," Miss Millie announced pointing dramatically to her short but glowing purple hair. "So I said to her afterward. Honey, maybe hairdressing isn't your thing."

Cory laughed again. She was so glad she chose to come to her grandmother's.

She felt warm and loved again in her arms. All it took was one knowing look and hug from her grandmother to ease some of her pain away. Instantly, Cory was able to forget her troubles and laugh out loud. Her grandmother could always weave that magic. She was the only one in her family who could get Cory to smile and laugh even when she was in her foulest or most depressed mood.

"Do you want me to fix you something to eat, Cory?"

"No, Gran. I'm fine. I bought dinner at the airport before I boarded. I believe my bed is calling me now."

"Well, I fixed up the guest room for you already. There are clean sheets and everything in there waiting for you."

"Thanks, Gran." Cory kissed her grandmother goodnight and settled into her new room for the next couple of days. She didn't know how long she would be hiding out here for. She switched off her cell and undressed. All she needed was a quick, hot shower and her pillow. She was way too exhausted. She didn't even want to think anymore.

Chapter 29

Cory awoke Saturday morning to an excruciating headache. That wasn't all, either. There were also the back pains. Maybe she slept badly on the tiny single bed in the room. It was only when she had to rush off the bed and dart into the bathroom to throw up, did she realize it was a hangover.

She knew there was a reason she didn't drink scotch. But that was the only alcohol in the apartment yesterday. And she had so desperately needed something to ease her pain. Now she was sick with an upset stomach and a banging headache. Cory didn't know why she was having the back pains, however. She needed some more sleep but the vomiting didn't want to end.

Miss Millie passed her throwing up in the bathroom sink. "Morning, sweetie. I brought you some soup."

"Good morning," Cory managed to get in over the sink before another mouthful of the fried chicken she ate the night before came gushing through her mouth in liquid form. She remained by the sink hugging it until she felt assured her stomach was completely emptied of all its contents.

"Eat some of this, you'll feel better," her grandmother coaxed her.

"Soup for breakfast?" Cory asked, puzzled. "Gran, I don't think I could get anything down my throat right now," she admitted. "I had too much to drink yesterday."

"You mean all of this is just from a hangover?" Miss Millie asked with concern in her voice.

"Yes, Gran! What else would it be?"

Miss Millie flashed a knowing look at her. "By the way, it's almost lunch time, sweetie. So eat up."

She left Cory to herself to try the soup. After only three spoonfuls of the steaming but delicious Tobago concoction, Cory couldn't have anymore. There was something riding her mind. At this point she had no other choice. She had to do it. She grabbed her handbag and started rummaging through it. She found what she was looking for and went into the bathroom again. This time she locked the door behind her.

Cory opened the box of the pregnancy test and read the instructions. She had bought it weeks ago when she missed her last period. She had been too nervous to even look at it since. She never bothered to tell Adrian because she didn't know how he would have reacted. She didn't even know how he felt about having kids because they never discussed it. She was planning to bring the subject up when they were at the beach today. Cory only now realized that they were supposed to be at Maracas this very moment, relaxing and enjoying the day. If only things didn't take such a drastic turn for the worse yesterday.

Cory paced the bedroom floor as she waited for the results. What an extremely bad time for her to be taking a pregnancy test, she thought. She didn't know how she was going to deal with a positive result. It would be so cruel of her to bring an innocent baby into this whole mess. Her marriage was in shambles. Everyone was probably mad with her in her family. Her friends. Jay. The only one she had on her side at the moment was her grandmother. Cory prayed to God for it to be a negative outcome.

When she finally mustered enough courage to look at the test result, she picked it up off the bed and read it. All her feelings and emotions instantly got the better of her. Relief and somewhat of a happy feeling of finally knowing coursed through her as she once again sank to the bed and sobbed.

Cory must have cried herself to sleep again, because when she turned and opened her eyes, her grandmother was sitting at the foot of the bed intently watching her. The pregnancy test was still in her hand but luckily for her, safely hidden under the pillow.

"Okay, Cory since you're up now, we need to talk, young lady," her grandmother had a stern look on her face this time. "I think I gave you enough time. So tell me what's wrong, sweetie."

This reminded Cory of being reprimanded as a child and that wasn't a nice thing. "Gran, nothing's wrong," she weakly muttered.

"So explain to me then, why you suddenly show up at my house in the middle of the night, wearing sunglasses. You practically slept through the entire day. You haven't eaten a thing," Miss Millie's eyes instantly darted to the now cold soup still sitting on the bed-side table. "Look at your eyes, they're swollen and puffy," she continued. "I may be old, Cory Mendez, but I'm no fool. And since you haven't mentioned your husband's name once since you've been here, I know this is all about him," she softened. "So did you two have a fight?"

"Yes, Gran," Cory quietly answered. "But it was a little more than that." She couldn't lie to her grandmother anymore.

"Well, I'm listening. I've nowhere else to go, sugar."

Cory took a deep breath as she sat up on the bed. She left the test hidden under her pillow. "Gran, what I'm about to tell you would be very disturbing and shocking to you. All I ask is that you please don't hate me for it."

"Cory, I'll never hate you for anything. I don't care what you did. Just tell me the truth," her grandmother said. "Okay?"

She began to tell her grandmother everything that happened as she knew it. From two nights before when Adrian was working on his computer game to when she showed up in Tobago last night. Miss Millie remained silent on the bed through the entire thing. She was visibly shaken and in shock after.

"Oh my Lord," was all she could manage to say, clutching her chest.

"Gran, are you okay?" It was Cory's turn to be concerned when she was finished talking.

"Yes. Don't worry, sweetie. We're going to be just fine." She gave Cory one last reassuring hug and got up to leave.

"Where're you going, Gran?" Cory asked.

"I need to think about all what you just told me here."

"Gran, I'm so sorry for all this."

"Sorry for what? Cory, this isn't your fault."

"Dad will hate me for this, though," she blurted out.

"No! I wouldn't let him," Miss Millie said indignantly. "Sweetie, why don't you go for a walk on the beach? Try to clear your head? It's such a lovely evening. Go get some fresh air, you'll feel much better."

"I think I'll do that, Gran," Cory announced as she climbed out of bed. She had been holed up in the house all day. She could really do with taking a walk and stretching her legs a bit now.

Chapter 30

Adrian was thankful. Thankful that at last one of his prayers was answered pretty quickly. Late on Saturday evening, his team was informed that their man, the same one they were after, had surrendered. He realized he would be tracked down so he did the sensible thing and he was now back in police custody. After he escaped the forests, he apparently walked into the nearest police station and just gave himself up.

This news could not have come at a better time for Adrian. As soon as they got it, everyone began organizing their equipment, weapons and gear and started the trek back out. At least their stint there wasn't a lost cause. Along the way, they found some marijuana fields and destroyed them. That would only mean less weed finding its way on the market.

When Adrian finally returned to the apartment late on Saturday night, it felt strange to him. It felt cold and empty and lonely. Although Cory's car was parked outside, the minute he turned the lock and stepped inside, Adrian immediately knew she wasn't there.

The apartment was too quiet. There was no laughter or giggles to soothe him. There were no delicious smells wafting through the air to greet his nose, either from her food or her signature scents of floral or citrus. None of these things greeted Adrian as he opened the door. He stared at an empty, cold apartment and was instantly reminded of the unhappiness and pain he'd caused Cory right there yesterday.

He dropped his gear and made his way to the bedroom. This only served to confirm his suspicions. Cory was gone. A golden glimmer on the bed caught his eyes. On closer inspection, it was something dear and precious to her. Her wedding ring. What was Cory's wedding ring doing on the bed?

As he sat on the bed and played with it in his hand, the cold, harsh reality became all too real for him to bear. Adrian sank into the bed and his entire world crashed before him. The woman he loved wasn't in it anymore. She left him and his worst fear had come true.

He was going crazy from not knowing where Cory was or what was going on with her. All sorts of madness rushed through his head. Adrian was becoming sick with worry. He grabbed his cell and dialed her number. It went immediately to her voicemail. He must have called her at least fifty times after that. She never once answered his call. He left just one voice message after all that.

Maybe he just needed to hear her voice again. No, that wasn't enough. How could that ever be enough? He needed Cory here with him, back in his arms again. He had to find her. Wherever she was, he had to find her. He had to make her understand that it was never his intention to hurt her. That he loved her with all his heart. That he couldn't possibly live here without her. In this apartment. On this island. On this earth.

Adrian needed a long cold shower but rushed out stark naked when he heard Pitbull and Chris Brown's "International Love" lyrics belting out. His cell phone was ringing. He didn't have time to see the caller flashing across the screen. He just grabbed the phone and answered. The first word to come out his mouth was, "Cory?"

"No, this isn't Cory. What's wrong with you? Didn't you see my number calling?"

"Oh, hi, Anna."

"Oh, hi, Anna? Is that all I get?" an irate Anna asked on the other end.

"I'm sorry. I thought it was Cory, okay?"

"Adrian, what's wrong?" Anna asked. "And don't tell me nothing because I'm hearing it in your voice. Where's Cory, Adrian?"

"I don't know, Anna. She left. I came home and she isn't here, okay," Adrian answered in a low voice.

"What do you mean she left? What's going on over there?"

"Look, Cory found out some things she shouldn't have. It should've come from me telling her personally. But now she knows and she hates me for it."

"What exactly did she find out, Adrian?" Anna persisted.

"Anna, I never even told you this before, okay."

"Told me what?"

"I can't be without her. I love her too much, Anna. But she doesn't want to even talk to me or see my face for that matter."

"Adrian, but what could you've possibly done to deserve that?"

"Remember when I asked you to pull that news clip for me? The one when Cory's brother was shot. I was there that night, Anna. I was part of the patrol unit that shot and killed four men two years ago. The driver of the car . . . that was Cory's brother. He was killed innocently. But we didn't know that, we had no prior knowledge that he wasn't a gang member or that he was even in that car."

"Hold up, Adrian. What're you saying?"

"I'm saying that I was responsible for killing my wife's brother," Adrian shouted through the phone. "But I swear I didn't know that before. But that's not what she thinks."

"Oh, God. So what does she think, then?" Anna asked in horror.

"She thinks that I deliberately lied to her and used her to hide the facts. She thinks I'm a murderer, Anna." Adrian paused after saying this. He still couldn't believe Cory called him that. "I had already fallen in love with her when I found out. What was I supposed to do? I know that I should've told her everything from the beginning. I know that. That was the biggest mistake of my life. I'm willing to take responsibility for it. But I just want to talk to her and tell her everything. I just need her forgiveness. But it's too late. She already left. I just want to see her again, Anna. I just want to hear her voice. I just want to hold her and comfort her."

"Adrian, I know you, okay. I understand why you felt you couldn't even tell me about this. Because you wanted to protect me. I get that. And I get that you didn't tell Cory because you didn't want to lose her. *Though it was stupid!* But I understand why you did what you did. And I know it couldn't have been an easy decision for you. But Adrian, you have to tell her everything now. Why you did what you did. That you love her and can't stand to be without her."

"Anna, I want to. But I don't know where she ran off to."

"So you're going to let that stop you? You just have to find her, Adrian," Anna was beginning to sound just as frantic as Adrian now. "You have to find her and tell her and make her understand. Use all your resources dammit. You just have to find her."

"I don't think that'll work, Anna. You know how stubborn Cory is. Besides she doesn't even want to speak to me."

"So that's it? You're just going to sit there and do nothing?" Anna's voice was now rising. "Adrian, I know you're a fighter and I know you love Cory more than anything in this world and I know you'll do anything, whatever it takes to win her back. So don't you dare give up now. I've seen you battle death. I've seen you battle terrorists. I've seen you battle loneliness. Now you have to battle for the woman you love and the life you want with her."

Now he would have two hysterical women to calm down and Adrian couldn't handle dealing with another frantic female on his hands again so soon. After a long silence, he finally broke it.

"Sis, thank you."

Anna laughed. "For what? I love you, bro. And I want you to be so amazingly happy. In fact, Adrian, since the first time I saw you and Cory together, I've never seen you so happy before. You're always there for me so all I need is for my one and only and most amazing brother in this whole world to be so very happy. You deserve it after all you've been through."

Adrian was glad his sister had put things into perspective for him. No matter what happened in the end, Adrian believed it was his duty to find Cory, tell her everything, and beg her to find it in her heart to forgive for all the pain and grief he caused her and her family. She deserved that much. Then maybe, he could go on from there somehow.

"Anna . . . I'm going after her."

Chapter 31

Adrian knew in order to find her quickly he had to start at the top. The top meaning him paying Cory's father a visit. He had sensed Jonathan Phillips disapproval of him but he was the least of his worries right now. Cory was his only priority. She was all that mattered at the moment.

Somehow, he had to suck it up and face the man again. And he had to take what he knew was coming to him like the man he knew he was. Adrian cringed as he remembered that night when he stood up to this man, in his own house. Adrian figured if he could face the wrath of drill instructors barking commands in his face and a grueling 365 days in Afghanistan, he could face Jonathan Phillips. Nevertheless, he prepared himself mentally for the battle ahead.

Knowing Cory, Adrian doubted she would be there. Though she loved her father to death and missed him terribly, he knew just because of what he did, Cory would never be able to face him again. That was the other reason why he had to do this. He had to at least try to get this family back together because he was the major reason it fell apart in the first place.

Collin was dead because of him. Cory and her father's now-strained relationship was because of him.

When he pulled up to the house that morning, he met Christian in the yard, busy washing down his father's car in the driveway.

"Adrian," Christian called out to him.

He had a big smile on his face. At least somebody was happy to see him, Adrian thought. "What's up, man?" Adrian asked. He walked up to Christian and bounced fists with him.

"I'm all right," Christian replied. "So what're you doing here? And where's Cory?"

Adrian's suspicions were right after all. Cory wasn't here and they didn't know where she was. He didn't know what to say to

Christian about the whereabouts of his sister. He was supposed to be her husband. The one protecting her, yet he himself didn't have a clue as to where his wife was.

At that exact moment, Jonathan Phillips chose to come out of the house, taking both Adrian and Christian by surprise. His hands were shoved in the pockets of the black shorts he was wearing, his bulging belly noticeably stretching his T-shirt to its limit.

"Adrian," Jonathan greeted him politely.

"Sir," Adrian responded.

"Could I speak to you for a minute?" Both men asked the exact question at precisely the same time. Then they stopped and just stared at each other, both wondering what the other wanted to say.

"Come inside," Jonathan announced. Adrian followed him, leaving Christian alone.

"Have a seat," Jonathan offered him. Adrian grabbed the one closest to him in the living room.

"Would you like a scotch on the rocks?" Jonathan again offered.

"Ah, no thank you, sir," Adrian declined.

Jonathan poured one for himself anyway.

Adrian cleared his throat and began immediately. "Um, I have some things I need to say to you, sir. First of all, I humbly apologize for disrespecting you in your home the last time I was here."

Jonathan raised his hand and immediately stopped him. "Wait! Before you say anything else, Adrian there is something I need to say to you first."

Here goes, Adrian mentally prepared himself for the coming onslaught.

"That wasn't disrespect. That was what I would call standing up to someone," Jonathan began. "Which was well warranted. So you have nothing to apologize for. I know that decisions for war and military orders don't come from the soldiers themselves. And believe me, if I were to ever go to Iraq or Afghanistan, I'd probably shit myself."

Adrian smiled at Jonathan's bold admission.

"Look, Adrian . . . I guess what I'm trying to say is that you're a brave young man. To do what you do or what you did on a daily basis. I don't think I could ever grow enough balls to do any of that."

This was another shocker for Adrian. He had come here prepared to do battle if he had to but Jonathan Phillips was taking a completely different approach to everything now. He was flipping the script just like that.

"This means a lot to me, sir. To hear this coming from you. Especially with all you and your family have been through," Adrian was being as sincere as he could be. "But there's something I came here meaning to tell you and if you can still say these words after, then I'll be eternally grateful."

He told Jonathan everything. From the fateful day he and Cory met, what really happened two years ago with the shootings, how he found out and connected the dots and how Cory eventually found out before he had told her anything, all up until the present with her disappearance.

Jonathan remained seated throughout the entire thing. He sipped slowly on his scotch intermittently but never interrupted Adrian. The two sat there with Adrian doing all the talking now but what Adrian noticed, surprised him the most. Jonathan Phillips didn't seem surprised at all by all this or fazed even, to say the least.

"Sir, you do understand the magnitude of all these events I just told you, right?" Adrian enquired.

"Yes," Jonathan answered simply. "Look, Adrian. I have to be honest with you here, too. Cory's grandmother called me yesterday. She told me everything. But from what Cory had told her, of course. I honestly believe that there are always two sides to a story. And now that I have heard your side, I have come to the conclusion that my son's death two years ago was an accident. As hard as it was and still is to take in, I have to accept it for what it is. And I appreciate you telling me all this, Adrian. Everything finally makes some sense now. I know it took a lot of guts for you to come clean and tell me this and I'm indeed thankful for it."

"Miss Millie told you this?" Adrian asked dumbfounded.

"Yes. Cory is with her now."

"Cory is in Tobago?" He was glad he now knew where she was. And that she was safe.

"Yes. She told me how Cory came to her. Let me warn you, she's really in a state. She really took this hard, her grandmother said."

"I know," Adrian answered quietly. "I have to go, sir. I have to talk to Cory. This is something I should've known better to do from the beginning." He immediately got up off the chair.

"Adrian, before you go. Just so you know my daughter is a very stubborn person. She took after her father," Jonathan added and smiled.

This was absolutely the very first time Adrian saw the man soften and smile. But he had no time to stay and chit chat anymore. He had to go after the most important thing in his life at the moment. He was heading straight to the airport. He had no ticket or clothes or a hotel reservation but none of that mattered right now. As long as he reached Miss Millie's house and speak to Cory, to get to see her, he didn't need anything else.

"Sir, thanks for your understanding in all this. I really hope there could be a fresh start for all of us," Adrian said to Jonathan as he turned to walk out the door.

"I was only trying to protect my daughter, you know," Jonathan announced. "But in the end I also only caused her pain. Hence, I'm a lonely man today. I lost my wife, my son and now my daughter because of my stubbornness and stupidity."

"You haven't lost your daughter. I'll personally make sure of that, sir. You also have Christian. And if all goes well, you'll have gained another son," Adrian offered.

"Well, good luck, Adrian," Jonathan said as he shook hands with him. "I hope things work out between the two of you. I really do. My daughter needs a man like you to love her unconditionally."

"Thank you, sir." And before Jonathan could say another word, Adrian was out the door.

Chapter 32

The heavenly smell of freshly baked ham filled her nostrils. Cory took a deep breath of the divine aroma as she opened the gate to the small house. The place smelled like Christmas. Only it was July. So maybe it was Christmas in July.

She followed the smell from down on the beach where she had gone to clear her head early that morning. She was feeling much better today. Her appetite was back because her stomach was viciously growling at her. And this was just the right kind of comfort food she needed.

When she entered the bright yellow kitchen, her grandmother was taking out some freshly baked loaves of bread she had in the oven. Cory's mouth was salivating, knowing fully well it was going to have a piping hot meal of bread and ham in a minute or so.

The majority of islanders would normally have ham only at Christmastime, as was the tradition. But Cory and her grandmother would soon be having it in the middle of July. This was just one of the many reasons why Cory loved her grandmother so dearly. She was so unconventional. A classic nonconformist. To hell with traditions and customs. Her grandmother ate and wore whatever she liked, whenever she liked.

She would be the one to wear another color besides black at a funeral because of her belief that a funeral was supposed to be a celebration. A celebration of the life of the person who passed. Everyone couldn't understand why she hadn't shed a tear at her only child's funeral. But Cory understood. That was just who she was.

Her grandmother had to deal with so many deaths in her lifetime. Her two husbands, her only daughter, her first grandson. She probably was fed up with all the tears. Yet, she was still here, living life to the fullest. Cory wished she could draw some of her grandmother's strength and courage to go on now. Her love of life. Her free spirit.

"Hi, Gran." Cory kissed her grandmother on the cheek.

"Hi, sugar. You're finally back from the beach? I thought you didn't want any breakfast again this morning."

"Nah. Somebody was baking and I couldn't resist anymore."

"Are you finally hungry, sweetie?"

"Famished! How did you know I was craving this, Gran?"

"Oh, lucky guess," her grandmother winked at her. "Sit, let me make you a sandwich."

"I'm so lucky."

"Don't be silly. Who else do I have to do all these things for? Besides, I love having to cook when I do have guests."

"Boy, I need to come visit you more often, then," Cory said as she pulled out a chair from the small dining set in the kitchen.

"Now why would you want to leave that handsome husband of yours and come all the way up here to see little old me?"

Cory's cheerfulness quickly vanished from her face. She grew serious now. "Gran, I told you what happened. What he did. He lied to me. And I don't know if I can ever forgive him for that."

"You know you can mention his name, Cory."

"I don't want to, Gran." Adrian broke her heart. No. Her heart was shattered in a million tiny pieces and Cory didn't know if she would ever find all the pieces or how long she would take to pick them all up and mend it back together again.

"That's not going to make you not think about him or forget what you two have together for that matter," her grandmother added knowingly. "So are you going to stay mad at him forever?"

Cory sighed heavily and sank further into her chair. "Look, Gran, everything he and I had together was all driven by his guilt. His proposal, the gifts, the flowers, everything, okay."

And she was so stupid to believe it all. She got herself so wrapped up and lost in all the nonsense. This unbelievable, whirlwind romance. She never once stopped to think or ask a question. Maybe it was his charm or his damn accent. His gentleness. Or was it the way he made love to her like no other man could. The way he protected her. What the hell was it that made her fall so damn hard for this man?

"Don't be a fool, Cory. Did you stop to think for one minute that he could have been driven by love? You know, I've been thinking about this all of last night. That man loves you, Cory. In fact, he wouldn't have done what he did if he didn't love you in the first place. He could have easily just dumped your ass and never see you again and move on with his life and left it at that."

"And you really believe that?"

"Yes, I really do. I think he only did what he did because he didn't want to lose you, Cory. And at some time or the other, you're going to have to talk to him. But most importantly, you're going to have to listen to him. Hear what he has to say, Cory."

"But he should've told me the truth, Gran. Let me decide what I wanted to do. Not take matters into his own hands."

Her grandmother looked up at her for a moment. She stopped slicing the juicy red tomato on the cutting board and looked at her intently. "And if he did tell you everything Cory, would you have stayed with him? Would you still love him and even married him?"

"Honestly, I don't know what I'd have done, Gran." Cory was still trying to figure out the real reason she ran away from Adrian in the first place. Was it because he was actually there when her brother was killed or the fact that he knew all the while and deceived her?

"My point exactly," Miss Millie stated and went back to her cutting board.

"All I know is that I trusted him with my everything and he abused and betrayed that trust. He deceived me, Gran. And it's just amazing to me that out of the one point three million people on these two islands, Adrian had to be the one to be there that night."

"Because he was supposed to be there, Cory," her grandmother stated quite matter-of-factly. "I honestly believe he made a mistake, Cory."

"Well, this mistake cost somebody their life. My brother's life was wrongfully taken in all of this. Then the facts of that were hidden from me."

Her grandmother handed a plate to Cory. On it was a thick juicy ham sandwich with lettuce leaves sticking out of its sides. "Mistakes are made everyday by everyone but lessons are supposed to be learned from them. Besides, it wasn't like he alone deliberately did it. So if I was you, Cory, I wouldn't let my brother's life go for naught."

Cory couldn't resist taking a bite in the sandwich her grandmother just prepared. She finally sank her teeth into the warm bread. "What do you mean by that, Gran?" she asked.

"You have found true love. Don't let this come between you and Adrian. Without Adrian, you would have probably still been with that boring fool in his skinny suits."

"Granny?" Cory laughed despite the seriousness of the conversation. "That's an awful thing to say. Preston is a lawyer. He has to wear suits."

"I know, but they're too small!"

"So Gran, if you never liked Preston, how come you never told me anything before now?"

"Oh, I never said I didn't like the boy, Cory. I just didn't like him for you, sweetie."

"And what about Adrian? Do you like him?"

"Oh yes. Without a doubt, you two were meant to be together. You can see so much love with you two."

"So you have no problems with him being a soldier, then?"

"Why should I? That's the man's job, baby. What's better than having a man who's willing to give his life to protect you everyday? Besides, by the looks of him, I'm sure he's incredible between the sheets, too," she winked at Cory with mischief in her eyes. "Child, anytime that man looks at you it's as if he wants to. . . ."

"Okay, Gran. That's enough," Cory raised her hand in protest, shaking her head. They both burst into loud laughter. Talking about her relationships with her grandmother was one thing. Cory wasn't about to discuss her sex life, too, even though her grandmother was right on point. Adrian was giving it to her just the way she wanted it, needed it and liked it. That was another thing. How could she ever find her way back into another man's arms again? Certainly not after the way Adrian possessed her body and it responded to him in a language all of its own.

"So what do I do now, Gran?" Cory sighed heavily.

"Sweetie, I can't tell you what to do. You have to feel it . . . from your heart. Maybe you should listen to your heart for a change."

"Well, there isn't a question about it. My heart tells me I love this man more than anything. My heart, my soul, my body . . . my entire being loves Adrian so much," Cory said as the tears started again.

"So there you go. Sweetie, I think this is your biggest lesson you're to learn yet. Forgiving the one you love."

"But how could I ever forgive him, Gran? Love alone just isn't enough sometimes."

"Then sometimes, it's all we may ever need, Cory. All this old lady knows is that your brother was taken so that you and Adrian could have a chance at real love and make each other truly happy. Both of you needed to find true love in order to heal from all your past heartaches."

"You really think so, Gran? That all sounds like a fairytale to me."

"Trust me, sweetie. The Lord knows what He's doing. He may work in mysterious ways but He sure knows what He's doing, Cory," she laughed.

And somehow, these crazy words coming from her grandmother just made perfect sense to Cory. If she had half as much faith as her grandmother did, maybe she just might make it through this mess sanely.

"By the way . . . when are you going to tell the man you're having his baby?"

Her grandmother's question completely threw her. Her eyes widened in surprise. The ham sandwich she was eating slipped from her hands, landing on the floor. How did her grandmother find out? She must have found the pregnancy test in the trash.

"How did you know, Gran?"

"Child, look at you. When was the last time you took a good look at yourself in the mirror? You're as ripe and full as a mango hanging on that tree outside. I just have to look at your face and I could tell."

What was it about these old women? They could always just look at someone and know they're with child.

"Besides the last time I saw you, your stomach was as flat as Rihanna's," her grandmother went on.

"Gran and what do you know about Rihanna?"

"I watch B.E.T. sometimes, sugar."

Actually, Cory wasn't that much surprised by her grandmother's admission. What else was there for her to do? Since Albert died, her time was now consumed with growing vegetables in her kitchen garden, crocheting, and going to church on a Sunday morning.

Cory really wanted to laugh but the tears continued to flow instead. "Oh, Gran." She started crying uncontrollably now. Her entire body rocking from the violent sobs overtaking it. "What am I going to do?"

"Well, the first thing you have to do is tell your husband he's going to be a daddy, Cory. He deserves to know that much."

"But what if he doesn't want this baby, Gran?" she sobbed. "We never spoke about having any babies before. I don't know if he even likes them."

"Don't you worry about that. He'll want this baby more than

anything else in the world. You know why?" she asked. "Because you're the mother."

Cory sighed heavily. "How am I ever going to get myself out of this mess this time?"

"This is not a mess that can't be fixed, sweetie. You have a gorgeous husband who loves you. You're going to be having his son or daughter in a few months' time. Hmm, this sure makes me wish I was twenty-six again. You know your mother had you when she was twenty-six, too."

"I know. I miss her so much, Gran. I wish she was here now."

"I know. I miss her too, baby. She was my only child. I always wished I was taken instead of her. So that she could have experienced these things. To have seen all of you get married. And see her first grandbaby. Then her second. And third."

"Hold up there, Grandma! Now I don't know about all that."

"Are you crazy child? Take me as a good example. I had only one and look what happened."

"That's because you couldn't have any more children, Gran. You can't beat yourself up over that."

"I know that. And that's why you and that healthy-looking husband of yours can stop around five or so. That'll make me very happy."

"Not in this world recession, Gran. I'm lucky to even have a job right now."

"The recession will pass eventually. You know we can talk and plan how much we want. But only He has the master plan. He's the only one that knows how many babies will pop out of you."

"Gran!"

"Jesus, Cory. You're a married woman now. You need to chill."

"That's it. I'm blocking B.E.T. from your cable lineup."

Chapter 33

As Adrian disembarked from the small Caribbean Airlines plane that brought him over to Tobago, one thing was on his mind. He had to find his wife and get her forgiveness. Somehow or the other. He wasn't banking much on anything else but he had to explain everything to Cory.

Adrian finally figured out his true purpose for returning to his homeland. It was to find the woman of his dreams. Cory was the love of his life and he was about to lose her. He had made a terrible mistake. But he wasn't going down without a fight. Hell, he was born to be a soldier. He was a U.S. Marine. He fought a war in Afghanistan in a combat unit. He fought against Taliban insurgents and their IEDs. He faced sand storms and the cold. So not without one final battle. One last fight. The fight of his life. No, the fight _for_ his life. And this was the single most important thing he ever had to do in his entire life and the hardest. Adrian prayed he wasn't too late.

He was here on the tiny island for a few hours only. He had no clothes or a hotel room booked. He was even lucky to get a ticket at the airport for today. Then he would be leaving the island. He had no idea if he would be taking his wife back with him. That would have to be her decision. He came here for one reason. To explain everything to Cory and beg her forgiveness. If he got that, he would have to move on from there. Somehow.

He drove to her grandmother's house in a champagne-colored Corolla he rented at the airport, and the closer he got to his target, the more anxious he became. Funny, the feeling reminded him of the last couple of days he had spent preparing to be deployed to Afghanistan. The anxiety, the nervousness. The feeling of knowing what you had to do but worrying over if you had enough guts to do it.

He pulled up to the sage green flats that belonged to Miss

Millie. She lived here all alone since her second husband passed Adrian had learned from Cory. He got out the car and opened the small gate and headed up the narrow walkway. This was his second time here. The first was for his wedding.

The house was quiet as usual, but the smell divine. The deep, rich aroma of curried crab was tickling his nostrils, tantalizing his taste buds as he approached. His stomach grumbled in reaction to the pungent smell of food wafting through the air. It had been a couple days now since he last had a decent home-cooked meal for that matter. Adrian knew he didn't want to see anything like mac 'n' cheese on a plate right now.

Cory's grandmother was in her kitchen garden to the side of the house tending to her vegetables. Adrian called out to her when he spotted her. Miss Millie waved and motioned for him to join her. She was busy picking tomatoes and hot peppers and throwing them into a straw basket on the ground.

Her purple hair gleamed in the late Sunday afternoon sun. It looked like an at-home hair color experiment gone all wrong to Adrian. He had to smile, though. Apparently, his wife wasn't the only one in her family with the crazy hair. When he first saw Miss Millie at their wedding, it had been blazing red then.

Seeing her again was bringing back a flood of memories for Adrian. A few weeks ago he was here on this very island getting married and enjoying his honeymoon. And what a honeymoon it was. He and Cory practically made love on every square inch of that villa. The bed, the floor, the shower, the hammock, the pool. Adrian missed her so much now. Seeing her, listening to her crazy ideals, touching her. Hearing her moans of pleasure. Hearing her scream his name. Hearing her rattle off her crazy Spanish when she climaxed. Adrian didn't see any signs of Cory around here now.

He had to bend really low to greet Miss Millie with a hug and a kiss. Surprisingly, she looked happy to see him. Relieved even, if he judged her facial expression correctly. He had become quite good at deconstructing facial expressions, a trick he had to master on the job for detecting suspicious criminal behavior.

"I knew I would see you here again before too long," Miss Millie greeted him in a friendly voice.

Adrian didn't expect her to be this happy to see him at all. He knew Tobagonians were known for their Caribbean charm and warm hospitality, but this? He was half expecting Cory's Granny going all gangsta on him, greeting him with a shotgun by the gate, yelling at him to step off her property or else she'd pump some slugs in his ass or something like that.

"It's so nice to see you again, Miss Millie."

"Oh, forget me. I know who you really came here to see," she said, laughing. When she saw the confused look on Adrian's face she explained to him that Cory's father had called her and told her to expect him.

"He did that?" a shocked Adrian asked.

"Well, it's about time you figured that crazy wife of yours was hiding out here with me anyway."

Adrian wasted no time. "Miss Millie, is Cory inside?"

"No, love. She isn't here right now."

So where the hell is she, then? As if reading his frantic mind, she told Adrian where he could find her. On the beach. He should have guessed. Luckily the beach she went to was a short walk down the street from Miss Millie's house in Black Rock.

"Come inside and have a nice cold glass of mauby first, Adrian. The place is so hot today."

But Adrian politely declined. "I'll have to pass on that, Miss Millie. I really need to talk to Cory now," he said, already hurriedly walking back from where he had come. That and mauby was one local drink he hated. The taste was way too bitter for his liking. He wouldn't mind some of that crab and dumplings though, the signature dish here and Tobagonians had the right kind of sweet hand for it. But he wasn't here for his stomach, either.

Adrian could tell from the sounds of the waves crashing onto the shoreline that they were huge. The sea was rough today and by the sound of them, he knew it wasn't good for Cory to be swimming in. He hoped she knew better and stayed as far from the water as possible. It didn't matter for him, he have had to swim in water worse than this before. He sighed. How was he ever going to get accustomed to her not being there? Who was going to protect her now?

He briskly jogged down the steps leading to the beach. This wasn't one of the more popular tourist ones on the island, so there weren't many people around. It should be pretty easy for him to spot Cory. His sneakers sank into the soft sand as he walked closer to the water's edge. His eyes combed the long beach and the waters like the trained soldier that he was. His light blue short-sleeved shirt fluttered in the strong wind. He also noticed the work of the sea, slowly eroding away the soil of the banks from where he stood.

Some young boys were busy playing a game of beach football further down the beach. Or as his American side of him would say, a game of soccer. This didn't surprise him. Football was the most popular sport here and school was out for the summer vacation. He imagined Dwight Yorke growing up on this his native island doing the same thing, before making it big time in England playing for the likes of Manchester alongside players like David Beckham.

The boys used pieces of twigs stuck into the wet sand as their goal posts. They were shouting and laughing. They were happy. Adrian remembered back in the day when he and his cousins used to do the same thing. Back then, he didn't have a care in the world. Now, he never dreamed he would be combing an entire beach, searching for the woman he loved.

It wasn't long before Adrian spotted her. He wondered if she made him out yet. If he had to chase her down this long stretch of beach today, he was prepared to do that, since she had developed a tendency of running away from him. Cory was walking toward him, her crazy hair blowing wildly in the coastal breeze. He was relieved. To find her. To see her after so long—two days that seemed like two years. To discover that her hair wasn't purple!

An artist's impression would paint an incredible picture of her. Cory never looked more beautiful. He watched as she walked down the beach, her body taking its sweet time to reach him. That was okay, he wasn't planning on going anywhere. She was draped in a deep red shawl to her knees, her feet being occasionally washed by the sand churning waves breaking onto the shore. She looked truly a sun-kissed island goddess now.

*

It was another scorcher of a day. Since she'd arrived in Tobago, this was the third time Cory had come to the beach to cool off and think. She had been to the beach earlier in the morning but after having breakfast and her grandmother leaving for church, she was all alone. That was when she had switched on her cell phone again. She had forgotten all about it. There were fifty-nine missed calls on the screen and all of them were from Adrian.

When she did listen to the one voice message he left, she was only left in tears again. They were both hurting so much. That was why she was here again. She needed another round of beach therapy. The wind and the sounds of the waves soothed her soul. Albeit, it defeated the whole purpose entirely. All she could think of was Adrian. She was immersed in his world after all. He loved the sea so much.

This afternoon, she just sat on the beach again thinking. Cory never ventured into the water at all since she was here. She wasn't a first-class swimmer like Adrian was and besides, the water was too rough for her to even try to swim. As she looked up from the white foamy sea caressing her bare feet, her heart did a double leap in her. Adrian. He came. He actually came after her.

It felt the very same way. The very first time she looked up into his eyes at the police station. The first time she went to see him at the military base. What seemed like ages ago. But this was all less than six months. Cory was incredibly happy to see him. The butterflies still danced and fluttered about her stomach. Or was that his baby, sensing his father was close by? Her hand instinctively went to her smooth belly and caressed it. She smiled inwardly.

He was standing there, watching her every movement as she neared. Cory instinctively clutched the shawl tighter around her body.

"Are you cold, baby?" the voice she loved to hear asked her. There was genuine concern etched in it.

Oh, God. She could do this. She had to do this. Cory never questioned that Adrian would go to the ends of the earth to protect her if he had to. The funny thing was, it had been him she needed protection from all the while. She didn't answer him, not trusting herself to speak. She wanted to say something but words failed her this time. For the first time in her life, words actually failed her.

She wanted to keep walking. It was too painful to look at him. She must stop walking. Her two feet kept on walking right past him. As she brushed past, Adrian held on to her arm, forcing her to finally stop. Then she looked at him. He was a man apart. His handsome face troubled. She could see the sadness in his eyes. She knew it was sadness instantly. It was the same reflection she saw everyday since she was here whenever she looked in the mirror, too.

"For a man with all your resources, you sure took a long time to find me," her words came out sounding bitter and cold.

Adrian completely ignored her comments.

"So who told you I was here?" she went on.

"That doesn't matter, Cory." His voice was low, he was sounding even softer than usual.

"It does to me. I want to know who sold me out," she snapped.

Adrian hesitated. "Your father told me, okay," he sighed.

"My father?" Cory asked incredulously. "But I didn't tell him about this."

"Well, your grandmother told him everything apparently."

"So that's why she asked me to take that walk," Cory whispered to herself. "Oh great. Now I'll never hear the end of this from him."

"I need to talk to you, Cory." Adrian was still holding on to her arm. It was a firm but gentle grasp. "There are some things I need to explain to you. Then I promise, I'll be gone, okay."

"Fine. So explain then." Her tone came across as surprisingly harsh to even her.

He led her over to the sandy steps he just came down from. She sat down.

He remained standing, shoving his hands into his pockets.

"Cory . . . I'm so sorry I put you through all this," he began. "I know I should've told you everything from the beginning but I was so insecure about losing you."

Cory could feel his agony resonating through his voice. It was so painful to listen to him speak.

"I need to tell you exactly what happened that night. Everything. I know how much your brother's death hurt you and I'm willing to take full responsibility for that. But there are just so many things that go on everyday that the average population doesn't know of." Adrian sighed out aloud again. "I know there's nothing I can do or say to bring Collin back. But you must know this, if I could, I'd bring him back for you, Cory."

They were already welling in her eyes since he started speaking. There wasn't anymore room for her eyes to hold them in any longer. They were all fighting to get out all at once. When Adrian said this to her, they started rolling quickly, all the way down. Passing her tanned cheeks, passing her quivering lips along the way as they traveled.

Finally, they dropped on her hands. They were hot. They were coming fast and furious now. She had to close her eyes, to force them back up somehow. These were the tears of anguish. She saw Collin in her mind smiling then. He was tugging her hair. Then he waved and ran away.

Cory felt her tears being wiped away. Her eyes instantly flew open. Adrian was sitting next to her now. There were some glistening in his eyes, too.

"You must believe this was also hard for me to deal with. I probably never told you this before, Cory. But to take somebody's life is never easy. And I hope to God you don't think that I enjoy doing that, even if they're really bad people. But it's even worse when they're good and completely innocent people. You go over and over in your mind if using lethal force is your only option. If you could have done something differently?"

He let out a little laugh. "But I'll be honest with you, when the barrel of a gun is pointing in your direction, it's either you or them. You see, baby, I know for me. I don't know about the others. Collin was the victim of a crime. But it really was an accident, Cory. I was there. Believe me, this is the truth. We had no prior knowledge that he wasn't a part of that gang, only after the investigations were carried out. He was proven to be completely innocent in all of this. In fact, he was the only innocent one in all of this."

Cory took her grandmother's advice and really listened to him this time. His story was different from what she had heard on the news, from what was reported in the newspapers. From what the police told her family. Yet, she believed his every word. She knew the truth finally. For the first time she knew what really happened to her brother that night. All her questions were finally answered. She could finally put her brother to rest in peace now.

Cory didn't expect to feel such a rush of relief wash over her entire being like that. Two long years she had been waiting on these answers. From the government, from the police. The truth finally came from someone she least expected to be there that night. From her very own husband. Should she feel grateful that Adrian was there? That she was given a firsthand account of the details from him? It was hard for Adrian to tell her these facts but he did. He sounded remorseful. He only wanted one more thing from her before he left.

"I know I'm asking a lot from you but can you ever find it in your heart to ever forgive me, Cory? For keeping the truth from you? For being involved in your brother's death?"

Cory was shaking. She knew her answer to this question ultimately decided how her life would go on. One with Adrian in it or one without him in it. A day without him was already like a day without light. A day without laughter. A day without music. A day without the ocean and birds singing, sunshine and rain. A day without air. What would an entire lifetime be like?

Cory clutched the shawl even tighter around her body. Her words came out sounding choked at first and they were already so hard to come by. "Everything happened so suddenly. All at once for me to handle. My brother, then my mom." She sobbed in between. "I had a nervous breakdown. I had to be treated by a psychiatrist. I went into a depression, Adrian. All this I suffered because of you. I couldn't go on anymore. This was the darkest part of my life I wished to forget. Everyday I thought it was a dream and then I'd wake up from it and my brother would be here still."

Cory was sobbing loudly between her sentences, between her words.

"Then I met you, Adrian," she went on. "I fell so completely in love with you. Then everything changed. I wanted to live my life again. Your love helped me to turn things around. To heal. It offered me solace and peace. I began to see so many things so differently."

Cory smiled as she wiped away the tears. Now it was her turn to talk and nothing was going to slow her. "I had finally put all that pain behind me. Then I find out the man I love so much was the cause of all my pain in the first place.

"I said, oh no. No way this crap could be happening to me all over again. So I ran away. I had to get away from it all. Maybe things weren't as they had unfolded I thought. I came here and I prayed. I went this over and over in my mind. But then I got the shocker of my life instead," Cory laughed despite herself between the tears. "All of this really had to happen for a reason, Adrian."

Adrian looked away. He was ashamed of himself but he never intended to hurt her. "Cory, I'm so sorry. I can't believe I put you through all this because of my selfish insecurities. I really wish I could erase all your hurts and pains. Especially the ones I caused you. But I'll understand if you can't forgive me. I know you'll never want to see me again or even speak to me directly after today. If you want a divorce and if you want to cut me completely out of your life, I can understand all of that too. I'll have to accept it. I'm willing to pay for the consequences of my actions."

"Is that what you think?" Cory asked him. "Look, Adrian in order for me to move on, I have no other choice but to forgive you," she said softly. "It's the only way I can come out of this whole mess sanely."

With relief etched over his face Adrian whispered, "Thank you." He closed his eyes and shook his head. "You have no idea how much your forgiveness means to me, Cory."

Then for the first time since she knew him, Cory saw tears roll from his eyes.

*

Adrian quickly got up off the steps. He didn't know how long they were sitting there talking. The sun was setting and it was growing dark. The huge black rocks jutting out of the water, probably from how the area got its name, looked even bigger and scarier now. They were the only ones left on the beach. He didn't even realize the boys playing football were all gone. When did they leave?

Adrian stooped on the steps facing Cory directly this time. He needed to let her know one more thing. "And baby, believe me when I say this. I never one day regretted asking you to be my wife. You were the most thrilling, refreshing thing to ever happen in my life. Being with you everyday felt like coming back home after an entire year of fighting a war." Adrian touched her on her cheek.

"The joy, the pride, the love." He was willing to take a slap if he had to now. "Of all I've seen in this world and been through in my lifetime, Cory, you're my most unforgettable moment. You made me love again. You made me dream of things I never wanted for myself before. Yet, you gave me more than I could've ever wanted or dreamed. I finally found peace within myself. And I thank you for all these things. So you must know I'll forever love you with all my heart, baby."

Adrian gently kissed her on her forehead. This time he had to go. Otherwise he would end up crying like a baby on this beach. He had gotten what he wanted. She offered him her forgiveness. For that, he was grateful. But why was he feeling so empty? She wanted to move on, she had said. He needed to walk whilst he still could. Adrian hopped up the steps, two at a time. He never turned around. If he only looked at Cory one more time he would crumble. All six foot plus two hundred pounds of him would just crumble in the sand.

Chapter 34

So that's it? No way in hell was Cory about to let the father of her unborn child walk out of her life just like that. This relationship was worth fighting for. Their marriage was worth fighting for. She refused to let him go.

"Adrian, wait!" she called. It was more like a frantic scream actually. Kind of like the one that had grabbed his attention at the police station. Cory's shout stopped Adrian dead in his tracks.

"There's somebody else . . . I need to tell you about," she said.

"There's somebody else in the picture," she said louder when he didn't turn around. Everything has changed, Adrian. That's why I can't let you go yet. I can't let you off the hook so easily."

This time Adrian turned around. "What did you just say?"

"I said I'm not letting you off so easily. I didn't go through two years of misery for naught." Cory was standing at the bottom of the steps now. "And I don't believe in divorces, by the way."

Cory removed the shawl draped about her shoulders. "I'm having your baby, Adrian," she blurted out. There, she said it. Now, she didn't know what to expect. Cory hoped this wasn't going to be another episode like when she had foolishly blurted out her love for him the very first time. Or the long silence that followed thereafter. They had never discussed having children in their short time together. But why shouldn't they have children? That was the norm after marriage. And this was a normal marriage founded on love, right?

"You don't want a divorce? Wait a minute . . . what did you say after that? I thought I heard you say. . . ."

"I'm having your baby," Cory finished for him. "Look at me, Adrian."

*

Then Adrian really looked at her. The shawl was gone. He noticed the round protrusion of her belly which used to be her flat stomach. A place he would normally shower with kisses. He just figured it was the weight gain she was complaining about these past two weeks. So that was why she had that shawl draped around her like that. That was why she had looked so different. Cory was pregnant all the while?

Adrian thought it was probably because he hadn't seen her over the last couple of days and that his mind was playing tricks on him. But Cory did look different. She was glowing. Her cheeks were rosy. Her skin was more sun-tanned and radiant than ever. Her breasts amazingly fuller under the black and white tankini she was wearing. Adrian had figured the island of Tobago most likely did this to her, the sun-tanned and rosy features. Her grandmother's cooking would have helped with the rest. He was still dumbfounded to say the least.

"What're you saying? How did this happen? When did it happen, Cory? You were on the pill, weren't you?" Adrian asked.

"Yes, but I sort of forgot to take them. Okay, I really skipped three days but then I took them afterwards . . . I guess that didn't work out," she laughed nervously.

Adrian shook his head. Only Cory would do something so completely nuts like that. But how wonderful that she did. Adrian bolted down the steps now.

"Why are you so crazy, Cory?" Crazy. Beautiful. Sexy. What else could he possibly ask for? He placed his hand on her rounded tummy, thinking of his child growing inside her for the first time. He had waited a really long time to hear these words. "You're really pregnant?"

"Yes. I took a test."

Adrian just stared.

"Well, say something, Adrian. Do you want this baby or not?"

"Cory, I'm sorry. I'm still in shock, baby," he grinned. Adrian had come here in hopes of her forgiveness with little expectations for anything more. He didn't have much hope that she would still want him back. But Cory didn't want a divorce. And to top it all, she was pregnant with his child. His head was spinning. He was so deliriously happy.

"Of course I want this baby, are you crazy? Cory, there's nothing more I'd like than for you to have my child. But are you sure about this?"

"Adrian, look how fat I am."

"You look so beautiful, baby. But what about us, Cory?"

"Well, I'm surely not going to raise my child as a single parent," she smiled. "Adrian, I'm so sorry for all those mean things I said to you. I love you so much."

"Baby, I'm so crazy about you," Adrian shouted as he gathered her into his arms. "Have been since I first saw you. You completely made my New Year. Then after I saw you screaming your head off at that police station again, it just sealed it for me. I love you, Cory. And I'm not going to let you go ever again."

Adrian kissed her madly. Passionately. He had his wife back and a baby on the way. His baby, finally. With the woman he loved more than anything. An enormous feeling of joy washed over him. Cory felt so good in his arms again. He thought of Collin. Somehow, it was he that had brought Cory and him together and Adrian owed everything he now had to his brave soul. He held her. She held him. They held each other for what seemed like an eternity on the beach.

"You actually came after me," Cory finally whispered against his chest, breaking the beautiful silence between them.

"Hey, I wasn't going to give up on us without one last fight." Adrian kissed her on her forehead. "I would have pursued you to the ends of this earth if I had to, Cory."

"Really?"

"You better believe it, baby."

Cory smiled up at him. "Could I ask you something, baby?" she asked.

"Sure, anything."

"How many kids do you want?"

"*What?*" Adrian exclaimed. "What kind of question is that?"

"Could you just answer it please?"

"Alright. Well, after I met you I decided that five was good enough for me."

"Five?" Cory questioned in wide-eyed amazement.

"Yep. Do you have a problem with that number?" Adrian joked.

Cory burst into laughter. "I don't actually. That'll make my grandmother really happy, though."

"Great. Just as long as she doesn't get any crazy ideas of coloring their hair purple or anything like that."

Cory cracked up again. "So what now, baby?" she asked.

"Well, let's see. I told you everything. You forgave me. You're having my baby. I missed you like crazy. So I suggest we go home now."

"Mmmm, home. That sounds real good to me." But neither of them could move from the beach. "Adrian, promise me one thing first."

"What's that, baby?"

"No more secrets between us."

"Look at me, Cory," Adrian pulled away to look her in the eyes. "Do I look like I'm crazy to you? That's it. No more secrets between us, baby. No way am I putting you through this again."

Things were finally looking up. It felt good to finally get everything out and tell Cory the truth. And to think he came so close to losing her.

"Okay, good. Now, let's go home, then," Cory cheerfully announced.

"Wait. First put this on," Adrian reached into his pocket and pulled out her wedding ring.

"My ring," Cory smiled.

"And baby, please don't *ever* take this off again," he chided.

"Sir, yes, sir," Cory saluted. Adrian slipped it on her wedding finger once more.

"Now we can go home, baby."

Cory and Adrian walked back to the house hand in hand. They could finally leave behind the turbulence and darkness that once threatened their love right there on that empty beach.

ABOUT THE AUTHOR

Heather Rodney-Diaz lives on the captivating twin-islands of Trinidad and Tobago in the southern Caribbean, indeed her motivation for writing romantic and super-sexy multi-cultural island escapes. Here, on these fascinating islands of sun, sand, and sea, there's no better place for dreaming up scorching hot heroes or falling in love. *Island Pursuits* is her debut novel. She'd love to hear from you. Drop her an email: *heather.rodneydiaz@gmail.com*, like her on Facebook: *http://www.facebook.com/HeatherRodneyDiazAuthor/* and Follow her on Twitter: *https://twitter.com/HeatherRodneyDi* and Pinterest: *http://pinterest.com/heatherrodneydi/*

www.ingramcontent.com/pod-product-compliance
Lightning Source LLC
Chambersburg PA
CBHW010637100726
47900CB00011B/2859